The text Luca read was from his team. As requested, the answers to his questions appeared in bullet points:

• A wife would go a long way to settling the unease in Madlena following Prince Pietro's death.

• News of Prince Luca's marriage would silence the naysayers, proving intentions toward Madlena are both serious and long-term.

• Arriving with a bride, followed by a formal blessing in the cathedral for everyone to enjoy, has been received with unanimous approval.

Good. It was his intention that he would be seen as a man determined to change. At some point in the future, when confidence in his reign was fully restored, his wife could be discreetly let go with his blessing and thanks, together with a healthy pension for life. Any children, if there were any, would stay with him. There would be no repeat of his brother's misstep.

• The magic of a royal wedding never fails...

Passion in Paradise

Exotic escapes...and red-hot romances!

Step into a jet-set world where first class is the *only* way to travel. From Monte Carlo to Tuscany, you'll find a billionaire at every turn! But no billionaire is complete without the perfect romance. Especially when that passion is found in the most incredible destinations...

Find out what happens in:

The Innocent's Forgotten Wedding by Lynne Graham

The Italian's Pregnant Cinderella by Caitlin Crews

Kidnapped for His Royal Heir by Maya Blake

His Greek Wedding Night Debt by Michelle Smart

The Spaniard's Surprise Love-Child by Kim Lawrence

My Shocking Monte Carlo Confession by Heidi Rice

A Bride Fit for a Prince? by Susan Stephens

A Scandal Made in London by Lucy King

Available this month!

Susan Stephens

A BRIDE FIT FOR A
PRINCE?

H HARLEQUIN
PRESENTS

HARLEQUIN®
PRESENTS®

Recycling programs for this product may not exist in your area.

ISBN-13: 978-1-335-14847-6

A Bride Fit for a Prince?

Copyright © 2020 by Susan Stephens

This edition published by arrangement with Harlequin Books S.A.

For questions and comments about the quality of this book, please contact us at CustomerService@Harlequin.com.

Harlequin Enterprises ULC
22 Adelaide St. West, 40th Floor
Toronto, Ontario M5H 4E3, Canada
www.Harlequin.com

Printed in U.S.A.

Susan Stephens was a professional singer before meeting her husband on the Mediterranean island of Malta. In true Harlequin style, they met on Monday, became engaged on Friday and married three months later. Susan enjoys entertaining, travel and going to the theater. To relax she reads, cooks and plays the piano, and when she's had enough of relaxing she throws herself off mountains on skis or gallops through the countryside singing loudly.

Books by Susan Stephens

Harlequin Presents

The Sicilian's Defiant Virgin
Pregnant by the Desert King
The Greek's Virgin Temptation
Snowbound with His Forbidden Innocent

One Night With Consequences

A Night of Royal Consequences
The Sheikh's Shock Child

Secret Heirs of Billionaires

The Secret Kept from the Greek

Passion in Paradise

A Scandalous Midnight in Madrid

Visit the Author Profile page
at Harlequin.com for more titles.

To all my wonderful readers, editors, publishing professionals, family and pets, who inspire me every day, and who make writing such a joy. Thank you!

CHAPTER ONE

HE ENTERED THE restaurant at the front. The young backpacker rushed in from the alley at the back. They met in the middle at the bar.

More accurately, she crashed into him.

'Sorry! *Sorry!*' she exclaimed, bouncing off him with a yelp.

'No need to apologise.'

He took stock of the new arrival. Bright eyes, firm chin and a face smudged with dust from her travels. It was an interesting face full of character and not unattractive. The impression of soft curves yielding to his muscular frame stayed with him as he stared into eyes the colour of an emerald ocean on an uncomplicated summer's day—which this should have been. But when was anything as straightforward as it appeared?

'I'm gagging for a drink of water,' she gasped to no one in particular. Turning to study his face with engaging frankness, she added, 'Do I know you?'

'I don't believe so.'

'Are you sure?'

He thumbed twenty-four hours' worth of stubble. 'As I can be.'

She continued to stare at him intently, as if his face rang a bell but her brain refused to yield the required information.

This break in proceedings allowed him to inhale her wildflower scent, and to appreciate more than a sweet rosebud mouth pursed in thought. Though, sweet was not a word he would use to describe her, he decided, noting the stubborn set of her chin and narrowed eyes as she ran his features through some internal search engine.

'I'm sure I know you from somewhere,' she insisted, still frowning. 'I just can't place you yet. But I will,' she warned with a smile that lit up her face. 'You're as out of place here as me, and yet you're totally relaxed…'

'Okay, Sherlock Holmes. Anything else?'

'You're obviously more used to eating in swanky eateries than I am…'

Undaunted by his silence, she turned to take stock of their surroundings. And gasped. 'Paint me staggered—I must have stumbled into Oz. Do people really drink magnums of champagne at midday?'

'It would appear so.'

She had freckles on her nose, he noticed as she wrinkled it with amusement. Having strayed off the alleyway behind the restaurant, she had landed in Babylon, where vintage wines were discussed in hushed tones, as if they were the answer to all the world's woes, while waiters served delicacies to clientele who, for the most part, couldn't care what they ate, so long as it was expensive enough to brag about. They were standing in a temple to excess on what was arguably the most stylish marina on the planet. He guessed the staff had left the rear entrance open to allow for the non-stop arrival of stock, as no place on earth could hope to keep sufficient food and booze on the premises to satisfy the appetites of the super-rich.

'Water and a job are what I need, and in that order,' the young woman announced, appearing to look to him for the solution. 'Do you know of anything going?' Chin angled to one side, she studied his face with brazen interest. Keen intelligence blazed from emerald eyes, and she had an eminently kissable mouth, he mused as she smiled again. 'Maybe I could get some work on board one of those huge boats in the marina…' She waited, and when he said nothing, she admitted, 'I've run out of funds. This trip has lasted longer than I expected. There's just so much to see, and so little time to fit everything in.'

'You're on some sort of deadline?'

'Not exactly,' she replied, 'but I do have to get back to work eventually—don't we all? I can't spend my entire life roaming. Though, I'd like to.' A wistful look crept into her eyes. 'At some point I've got to stop travelling and make a go of things again…'

'Again?' he probed as she stared off into the middle distance.

'Oh, you know what I mean,' she insisted with a careless flip of her wrist.

'I'm not sure I do. Have you travelled far?'

'From London, originally.'

'Where you live and work?'

She didn't answer his question, her gaze sweeping the marina. 'I adore the South of France, don't you?'

As attempts to change the subject went, that was clumsy. 'The Riviera's one of many places I like to visit.'

She pulled him up on his apparent disinterest right away. '*Like?* How can anyone *like* the South of France when it's so obviously gorgeous and fabulous? Don't you feel doubly alive when you're here?' Her face lit up, and all the tension he'd detected when she'd first burst into the bar dropped away. 'Music, food, heat, blue skies and sunshine—the way everyone throws back their shoulders and speaks out clearly instead of mumbling. People walk tall here with confidence and optimism, instead of huddling beneath raincoats in a grey, chilly drizzle—'

'You put forward a good case,' he conceded, shaking himself out of his black mood. 'Are you a lawyer?'

'No, but I've often thought legal skills would be useful.'

'In what way?'

'Oh, you know,' she said vaguely.

'If not a lawyer, are you a writer? Your descriptive skills?' he prompted.

She laughed and looked away.

'Why don't you ask here about jobs?' he suggested.

She swept a hand down her crumpled clothes.

'Like they'd hire me looking like this! And, anyway, I want to get as far away as I can. Out to sea would be my preference.'

'Are you under pressure to get away?'

'What makes you say that?' she asked quickly.

'I'm just following the ball of string as you reel it out.'

'So I'm not the only detective. I'd better be careful what else I say.'

'You'd better,' he agreed as measuring glances flashed between them.

Young, attractive, intelligent and feisty, she was a welcome distraction on a difficult day.

'I'm guessing you don't work here,' she said as she gave him a comprehensive once-over. 'Ripped shorts and a sleeveless top don't suggest to me that you're trying out for the job of waiter.'

'Me?' He laughed. 'No. I don't think they'd trust me at the sink.'

'A pot carrier, perhaps?' she mused. 'You've got the muscles for it.'

'I'm hired, then?' he teased with the lift of a brow.

'You wish.'

When she laughed a dimple appeared in her cheek, he noted.

'So how come they let you in?' she asked with an appraising look.

'Like you, I just walked in. If you do so with confidence, I find no one will stop you.'

'But you can't help me with a job?'

'Sorry. I'm afraid I can't.'

'Afraid?' she demanded askance. 'I've known you less than five minutes, but it's long enough to know you're not afraid of anything.'

He might have agreed with her at one time, but when the rock he'd built his life on tottered and splintered into pieces, all bets were off.

'Maybe you're the type of guy I should know better than to talk to?'

'Yet, here we are.' Making himself comfortable against the wall at the side of the bar, he spread his hands wide.

'Not for long,' she said briskly. 'All I need is a glass of water and then I'm out of here. I bet the barman could see you above their heads,' she hinted as she took in the crowd at the bar. 'Please,' she begged. 'You make the other men look like shrimps. They'll part like the Red Sea when they see you on the move. They wouldn't even notice me jumping up and down.'

'You flatter me.'

'Do I?' she demanded, opening her eyes wide. 'Entirely unintentional, I assure you.'

'All right,' he agreed. 'Stay there.'

'I'm not going anywhere without a drink of water,' she assured him.

She amused him, and had stormed his reserve with nothing more than a bold line in chat and an engaging smile. The pert breasts didn't hurt. Nor did a taut butt, displayed to best advantage beneath tantalisingly short shorts. It was all too easy to imagine those coltish legs wrapped around his waist, though they were tipped with a pair of battered old boots, which were possibly the ugliest he'd ever seen. He glanced back as he waited at the bar. Her face was a picture of puzzled concentration. She was still hammering away at the computer in her mind as she attempted to place him, he guessed.

Even windswept, she was beautiful. Smudged with dirt from the trail and make-up-free. Her hair, in particular, was an abundant, fiery magnificence. Its unusual shade of copper reminded him of sunset at sea. Held back carelessly with a few pins, it begged to be set free so he could tangle his fingers through the lustrous locks as he eased her head back to kiss his way down the long, slender line of her neck. But it was more than good looks that had captured his attention. She had character and spirit and gave as good as she got, which, in the world of sycophants he was about to inhabit, made her a welcome change.

He was on a deadline. Soon he would return to the principality of Madlena to take the throne after the death of his brother. The responsibility that entailed hog-tied him a little more each day. This might be his last trip on his yacht the *Black Diamond* before duty put an end to his freedom for good. The last thing he needed was a complication in the form of a sassy young woman with a seemingly bottomless pit of questions. No doubt sex would ease his tension, but his usual pick would be an older, experienced woman who knew the score, not an ingénue on a backpacking trip around Europe.

'Water! At last!' she cried theatrically as he handed over a misted bottle and a glass.

As she reached for it, her body brushed his, causing a riot she was seemingly unaware of, while his groin had tightened to the point of pain.

'Thank you,' she gasped on a grateful exhalation as she drained the glass.

'You could use another?' he guessed.

'You read my mind. But don't worry. I can handle it,' she assured him.

'Go to it,' he invited, standing back.

As she'd pressed against him, he'd been given more than a clue about the body beneath her shabby clothes. His adored *nonna*, Princess Aurelia, might have said this young woman was 'well made'. Although she was tiny like his grandmother, at least a head smaller than anyone else at the bar, which meant her repeated attempts to attract the barman's attention were a massive fail.

'All right,' she conceded finally. 'Seems I've got no option but to throw myself on your mercy again. Go to it!' she urged. 'I'll cheer you on from the sidelines—as much as I can with a throat that feels like sandpaper.'

Her voice was unmistakeably British, while her mouth was extremely sexy. An almost perfect Cupid's bow, it tugged up at one corner, which made the endearing dimple appear in her cheek. 'Hurry,' she begged, clutching her throat like the leading light in some amateur dramatic society. 'Can't you see I'm desperate?'

'You belong on the stage,' he commented dryly.

'Yeah, scrubbing it,' she agreed.

That she made him laugh on a day when laughter had seemed impossible pointed up the fact that this was no overentitled drip. She wasn't helpless in any way. Here in this preserve of the rich and famous, where labels didn't just count, they were mandatory, and where a designer outfit would never dare to show its face twice, she was as poised as a princess—and a lot more fun, if the selection of po-faced contenders drawn up by his royal council was anything to go by. She could also be a lot more trouble, he considered on his return from the bar. Her mouth had pursed disapprovingly when she saw him served before anyone else.

'I didn't ask you to crash the line,' she scolded with a grin.

'I didn't. The barman just happens to be super-efficient.'

'Okay,' she conceded. 'Well, thank you. You've done me a real favour, and I appreciate it.'

'I splashed out on two glasses of water,' he pointed out, bringing her back down to earth. 'Hardly a good enough reason to throw yourself at my feet.'

'You should be so lucky,' she assured him. 'Anyway, sometimes a glass of water is all it takes. Do you know everyone here?' she added as she glugged it down.

'No. Why?'

'Because they're all staring at you.'

'Perhaps they're staring at you.' When he turned,

heads swivelled away as the übersophisticated clientele pretended they hadn't seen him.

'Hmm,' she mused thoughtfully. 'I don't think so.' She downed the second glass in record time. 'I'm well outclassed.'

That was a matter of opinion.

'Anyway,' she added with a gasp of relief as she put the empty glass down, 'don't let these nosy parkers worry you. You've got me to protect you now.'

'That's a joke?' he asked.

'Take it any way you want,' she said, 'but my suggestion is, just ignore them.'

Fiery hair was a fair indicator of temperament, he suspected, guessing she could be a little terrier if she was put to the test. There was no risk of overdosing on sugar when it came to this woman.

'So,' she added, barely pausing for breath, 'are you going to tell me who you are? I mean, apart from being the only person in here as badly dressed as me?'

There was no denying they were both showing a flagrant disregard for the dress code. As a minimum, patrons were required to wash the sand from their bodies before sitting down to eat—but who questioned royalty? And she was with him.

'My name is Luca,' he revealed. 'And you are?'

'Before we get to that—' she gave him one of her cheeky smiles '—I want to know how you've managed not to be thrown out when you look as if you've just stepped out of the sea.'

'Because that's exactly what I did.'

'Okay…' She drew the word out. 'My best guess, in that case, is that even if they combined their forces, security and the staff here wouldn't dream of taking you on.'

'More compliments?' he suggested dryly.

Pressing her lips together, she grinned. 'My mistake. But you still haven't told me how you get away with it.'

'Perhaps they like me here, and make an exception?'

'And perhaps pigs might fly,' she countered dryly. 'The maître d' looks like a regimental sergeant major, and I don't imagine he lets anyone slip by. You're either respected or feared,' she conjectured. 'So, which is it, Luca?'

Probably a bit of both, he mused. 'I have been here before,' he conceded.

'So are you crew from one of those floating office blocks?'

Following her stare to the line of gleaming super-yachts moored up in a row down the quay, he shook his head.

'Not crew,' she reflected, 'yet everyone seems to know you, so are you the local criminal mastermind, or some fabulously wealthy billionaire out slumming it for the day?'

He raised a brow. 'I imagine I could play either role.'

'I bet you could,' she agreed. 'But not with me.'

'Has it occurred to you that it might be you that everyone's staring at?'

'Me?' she scoffed. 'I hardly fit the style brief here.

Apart from a few disapproving glances when I first walked in, no one's looked at me since.'

'Your fabulous hair might cause comment.'

'Why, thank you, kind sir,' she said, dipping into a curtsey.

'Did I let a compliment slip past me?' he mocked lightly.

She twisted her mouth before carrying on with her interrogation. 'It's definitely not me they're looking at. Now I've had my drink there's nothing desperate about me to suggest some sort of mystery attached to my coming here, or that might lead anyone to believe I'm seeking sanctuary in this steel and glass temple to excess.'

Sanctuary? '*Are* you running from something?'

Instead of answering his question she went off on another tangent. 'The trouble with Saint-Tropez is that it's so misleading. I'd never been here before, so when I first arrived it was hard to believe the town retained the charm of the original fishing village. There's such an abundance of megayachts and boys' toys—the dream cars,' she explained. 'But everything coexists happily. Bourgeois French life cheek by jowl with ostentatious wealth.'

'Don't you approve?'

'Of course I do. The contrast is what makes Saint-Tropez so special and fun to visit. But don't change the subject. We're talking about you.'

'*I* changed the subject?' he challenged.

She shrugged and laughed this off. 'So, come

on—tell me. Are you a celebrity, or a fugitive from the law?'

'I don't fall into either category.'

'You might as well come clean. I'm very good at extracting information,' she told him with a comic accent.

'MI6?'

'I've always fancied being a sleuth,' she admitted, adding a comic face to the mix. 'I could never resist a good puzzle.'

'Perhaps I'm hiding out like you.'

'I'm not hiding out!'

The heat of her defence reinforced his growing belief that that was exactly what she was doing.

'You could hardly blend into the scenery with your looks,' she commented, making it sound like the worst insult possible. 'Simply stating facts,' she told him when he raised an ironic brow.

Some women simpered and preened when they met him. She did neither, but continued to stare at him narrow-eyed, as if he were an interesting specimen in a lab.

'The name Luca isn't much of a clue...'

'Can you put a name to everyone you meet?'

'Of course not, but I really feel I should know you,' she mused, still frowning. 'Anyway, let's forget that for now. I'm on my own, trekking around Europe, so I'd better be careful who I talk to. I think it's time to move on.'

'That's your choice, but if you're so concerned

about safety, why strike up a conversation with a stranger in the first place?'

'You look trustworthy, and you don't frighten me.'

'Evidently,' he agreed, finding it hard to curb a smile.

Where had she been these past few months when his image had been splashed across the press? The tragedy of losing his older brother had resonated across the globe. First his grandmother, and then Pietro had raised him when their parents were killed in an air crash, only for Pietro to die in tragic circumstances. Two brothers cruelly torn apart, with the added fascination of great wealth and royal lineage, had made sure that their story reached everyone's ears.

Seeing him out of context must have thrown her. He bore no resemblance to the solemn man in uniform that had been pictured in the press. Those images showed a grim-faced individual, mired in sorrow, standing on a parade ground to accept the fealty of troops who were loyal to him now. That man didn't relax, or slouch on one hip, but stood sternly to attention, as he endured the unendurable, which was to accept that his beloved older brother would never brighten his life again. The diners who knew him here thought only that he was an aristocrat and a billionaire, with a megayacht worthy of mention. His vast three-mast rigger, the *Black Diamond*, was anchored off shore. Its modern take on a traditional design always caused comment, though no one fussed over him, as billionaires and members of the aristocracy were two a penny in Saint-Tropez.

The yacht was his pride and joy, and a guaranteed escape route from a news-hungry world. He'd bought it some years back with profits from a tech company he'd started in his bedroom as a boy. News had spread quickly that the Pirate Prince—as people liked to call him, thanks to his uniquely sinister yacht with its black sails and night-dark hull—was indulging in one last round of freedom before embarking on a life of royal circumspection.

'Since you're not afraid of me,' he told the young woman, 'I think it's time we became properly acquainted.'

'I'm honoured,' she mocked, bringing her hand palm flat to her magnificent breasts. 'My name is Samia. Samia Smith.'

'Exotic,' he commented.

'Me, or the name?' A smile tugged at her lips.

'What if I said both?'

'I'd say you were trying too hard and I don't think that's you.'

The name suited her perfectly. A bunch of contradictions, Samia was resolutely upbeat, but there was no mistaking the shadows behind her laughing eyes. 'Samia,' he murmured. Having tried the name on his tongue he found it rolled off like warm, sweet honey, much as she'd taste, he imagined. 'Very pleased to meet you, Samia Smith.'

'Also very pleased,' she said as they shook hands. She spared him another curtsey. But had she placed him, he wondered as she narrowed her eyes to stare thoughtfully into his. And would it change her attitude towards him if she had?

His best guess was no.

CHAPTER TWO

SAMIA'S TINY HAND in his big fist felt unreasonably small. Her grip was strong, her skin smooth and soft, as if she didn't work with her hands. She was in no hurry to remove her hand from his, he noticed, but stared directly into his eyes, giving the distinct impression that this was a woman who would bow her head to no man. Though, those shadows pointed to an event in her past that had driven her to travel in search of something different. Adding to his suspicions, there was a telltale mark on her wedding finger. A strip of pale skin showed where she had once worn a ring.

Forced to take hold of her shoulders to steer her away from a stream of waiters emerging from the kitchen, he was shocked by the bolt of heat that shot up his arm. This was matched by Samia's sharp inhalation of breath. As they swung around to stare at each other, something changed between them. No longer two strangers who'd met in a bar, they were a man and a woman reduced to their most primal state. There was a pulse beating rapidly in her neck, and her eyes were almost black, with just a thin rim of emerald around pupils grown huge. Some of the diners had noticed this bombshell, and were whispering about it, so he backed her into the shadows where they could talk unobserved.

'You don't want to be seen with me?' she challenged with a laugh.

'I don't want either of us to get in the way of the waitstaff,' he argued.

Of course there was another reason. Everyone with a smartphone was a member of the paparazzi these days, and shots of the Pirate Prince were priceless. How much more so, when the man in question appeared to be on the point of embarking on yet another affair? This was not the sort of thing he wanted his countrymen to see. They'd had enough upheaval, and must already be dreading the day when Prince Pietro's demon brother moved back home to take the throne.

'What brings you to Saint-Tropez?' he asked Samia. In unguarded moments, there appeared to be more than a backpack weighing her down.

'The name Saint-Tropez is magical, thanks to the film star Brigitte Bardot, who was just eighteen when she married the dangerously handsome Roger Vadim back in the fifties. They were lovers before I was born, but everyone knows their story and how they brought glamour to a small fishing village in the South of France. Who could resist that story?'

'Me,' he said bluntly. 'I see the place for what it is—a bustling, successful town.'

'You're a realist,' she confirmed.

'And you're a romantic, it would appear.'

'What's wrong with that?'

'Less than five years after they married, your glamorous couple divorced.'

'Don't spoil it,' she scolded. 'Why can't you think about the happiness they shared instead?'

'Because, as you pointed out, I'm a realist.' But he did enjoy this woman's company. 'Doesn't your romantic life ever hit the skids?'

'Can we remain on topic, please?'

Her expression changed. Blood drained from her face. The dreamy expression had left her eyes. She looked almost frightened. 'What can of worms did I just open?' he enquired, pinning her with a shrewd stare.

'The one that says I'm hungry as well as thirsty…'

He didn't believe her for a moment, but they'd only known each other five minutes, which was far too soon for true confessions. 'How much time did you spend planning this trip?'

'It was a spur-of-the-moment decision,' she admitted.

'Who doesn't need a time-out occasionally?' he agreed. By taking things slowly, he might find out more about her.

'I'm happy to go wherever the wind takes me.'

He didn't believe that either. Everyone had some sort of plan. As she glanced at the door she'd used to come in, he wondered if she was running from something…or someone, and if the mark from the ring played a part in that. She hid it well, but she was jittery, reminding him of one of his highly strung polo ponies: always loyal, always willing, always ready to bolt. Beneath Samia's engaging personality, there was a story, and he wanted to know what that story was.

'So you always make a plan before you do anything?' She raised a brow. 'In that case, why should I believe that you just happen to be here, propping up the bar without good reason?'

If he told her he'd come to meet the man who had adopted his brother's child, would she believe him? Both the surrogate his brother had used and her husband wanted nothing from Luca, other than for him to know that his dead brother's child was safe and loved, and that they would never put a claim forward to the throne of Madlena.

Why would they? Maria, the child's mother, had demanded. Who in their right mind would choose to be royal?

Who indeed? he'd thought at the time, knowing only too well the restrictions that would place on the child.

Maria had decided not to go through with the surrogacy, she had explained, and had told his brother this before Pietro's death. Her husband was in full agreement. The child was theirs and needed no royal connections to improve his lot. What had hurt Luca the most was that Pietro hadn't felt able to share his longing for a family, and he blamed himself for being away while his brother had nursed this sad wound. All he could do for Pietro now was to keep his brother's secret. The people of Madlena needed reassurance, not another upheaval. 'I came here to settle some family business,' he told Samia.

'I think you're a bit of a romantic on the quiet,' she observed, smiling warmly. 'Family is—or should be—everything.'

There was a wistful note in her voice as she said this. 'It is to me,' he confirmed, more curious than ever about her backstory.

'Are you far from home? Judging by your accent, you're not French.'

'I sailed here,' he reminded her, 'I could have come from anywhere, but I guess my voice and my name tell their own story?'

'It's more about the tone of your voice,' she mused, eyes half-closed. 'Rich dark treacle with husky bass overtones…'

A laugh burst out of him. 'If I had a clue what you're talking about.'

'Just hum, but don't commit yourself,' she advised, eyes flashing open to spear him as she spoke. 'That's what I do when I don't want to answer questions—and it's obvious you're about as interested in answering questions as I am.'

'Point taken,' he said, interest spiking again as they stared into each other's eyes.

'I'll stop talking now,' she said, resting back against the wall next to him.

'Is that a promise?'

She turned her head. 'It's as close as you're going to get.'

The fact that they were still talking was nothing

short of a miracle. Since Pietro's death, he'd had no patience for anyone or anything. Discovering his brother had wanted a family so badly, yet had not mentioned this to Luca, had rocked his selfish world on its axis. How could he have been so self-absorbed he had remained oblivious to his brother's distress? He had a lot to learn if he was to avoid letting down his country, as he'd let down Pietro.

'Where are you heading when you leave here?' his companion asked.

He turned to face her. 'I thought you promised not to talk.'

'It wasn't a forever promise, and you look as if you need a distraction.'

He smiled in spite of himself. There was something about Samia that forced him to see a lighter side of life. It also made him want to kiss that cheeky mouth into silence.

'Are you going home soon?' she prompted.

Home to him was either on board his sailing yacht, or on a bunk in a spartan barracks. A sumptuous palace with servants waiting on him hand and foot was his least favoured choice. That had been his brother's life, while Luca had joined Madlena's special forces where he had believed he could be of most use to his people. He had never imagined his parting from Pietro would be so final, or that the memories they'd shared would be tainted by the pain of knowing he'd let his brother down.

'You look sad and angry,' Samia commented with

a frown. 'Is that my fault? Have I said something to upset you?'

'I'm not sad.'

'I'm pleased to hear it. Being Italian can only be a cause for celebration.'

He wavered between wanting to leave and ending their encounter, and staying to allow Samia to distract him from memories of his brother that threatened to splinter his mind. When his grandmother had been widowed and had gone off to live her own life, Pietro had raised him and cared for him, and where had he been when Pietro had so badly needed him?

'All that delicious pasta—'

'What?' His tone was harsh. Samia's intrusion into his private grief had jolted him—and even that was an indulgence. But seriously. Pasta? Of all the things she could have said about Italy—the art, the music, the architecture and stunning scenery—in her uniquely uninhibited way, she had gone straight for a decent plate of food. With a wry huff, he shook his head.

'There you are, you see,' she asserted. 'You're not so grim, after all. And I bet you're as hungry as me...'

'Are you hungry?'

'What do you think?' she teased. 'But I don't have enough money, and there's no chance we'll get fed here, even if I could afford it. With the best will in the world, the maître d' couldn't find us a table.'

He didn't disillusion her, though he only had to raise a brow for a table to be made instantly available.

'We're sunk,' she said.

'*We're* sunk?' he queried.

'Of course *we*. I'm hungry and you must be too. After your swim,' she reminded him.

Okay, he did have an appetite, and not just for food.

'Hamburger?' she suggested.

He followed her gaze to the public promenade where a hamburger stall was placed conveniently in the shadows.

Momentarily distracted as a text pinged on his phone, he saw that it came from the head of his PA team in Madlena. A Red Box, that indispensable piece of royal equipment designed to hold documents relating to vital matters of state, would be delivered to his study on board the *Black Diamond*.

He texted back.

I'd like you to look into something else—someone else.

Key points only, he added, after printing Samia's name.

'Finished?' she asked with a mildly disapproving look as he stowed the phone back in his pocket.

'My world never sleeps.'

'Poor you,' she said as he turned for the exit.

'I thought you were hungry. Aren't you coming with me?'

She shrugged and held back. 'I don't know you from Adam. Perhaps I should split.'

'Only you can decide. Are you hungry or not?'

'Hungry, but—'

'But what?' he demanded impatiently.

'If I do come with you, you have to take this.'

He stared at the ten-euro note she'd pressed into his hand.

'I know what things cost in this town,' she insisted. 'Great for keeping your ear to the ground, but not for eating out.'

'You're not a newspaper reporter, are you?'

She laughed. 'Why, do you have something to hide?'

'Do you?'

'Now we're both intrigued.' A smile hovered on her lips as she gave him a sideways look.

Warning bells started clanging loud and clear. Base instinct drowned them out. They had started leaning towards each other as their discussion grew more heated, close enough for him to detect Samia's wildflower scent, and to absorb the warmth of her body.

'I don't know how you can look so serious,' she told him. 'I find it impossible not to smile in Saint-Tropez.'

But with shadows in your eyes, he thought as she added, 'The sun is shining and the sky is bright blue. What's not to like?'

'A woman who never stops asking questions?' he suggested.

She laughed as she swung her bulky backpack off the floor, almost taking out a couple of drunks. Fortunately, they were too far gone to notice.

'I guess sailing isn't just work for you?' she said as she wove her perilous way through the crowded tables.

He glanced outside to where the bay of Saint-Tropez lay tranquil and glistening like a bright blue disc sprayed with silver in the trembling heat of late afternoon. 'No,' he agreed, remembering long, silent nights at sea beneath a blue-black sky littered with stars, and crazy, windy sunlit days when dolphins raced ahead of the prow. 'Sailing isn't just work for me.'

'No wonder everyone's staring at you,' she commented when they reached the exit. 'They're jealous as hell, and I am too. What a wonderful life to work on board a yacht. Is the yacht where you work in the marina? Can we go and look at it when we've had something to eat?'

'It's moored out at sea.'

'Oh.' She sounded disappointed. 'Which one is it?' Shading her eyes, she followed his gaze. 'You are kidding? You work on board the *Black Diamond*? Everyone in town is talking about it. Isn't that one of the biggest sailing yachts at sea?'

'*The* biggest.'

'I read an article about the *Black Diamond*. If you could get me a job on board, it would be a dream come true.'

'I can put in a word.' It wasn't such a bad idea. A distraction like Samia was exactly what he needed before returning home to take up the reins of duty.

'I'm impressed,' she admitted. 'All the other yachts

are scrubbed white to within an inch of their plim-soll line, while you sail the devil's own invention.'

'It's black,' he agreed.

'And massive.'

'Larger than average,' he agreed dryly.

'I'm glad you don't work on one of those float-ing office blocks.'

'But rather the stuff dreams are made of?' he sug-gested with a cynical lift of his brow.

'Where I'm sure you fit right in. The pirate look?' she prompted. 'You're only short of an earring and a parrot on your shoulder.'

Game on, he thought as they stared at each other and laughed.

CHAPTER THREE

SAMIA FROWNED AS she weighed the evidence. 'How did you get from ship to shore?'

Luca shrugged. 'Swam from the deck.'

Her frown deepened. 'That explains the thin film of sand on your skin.'

'You're quite the sleuth.'

'Just interested,' she admitted. 'But, surely that deck's too high for you to dive safely into the sea?'

'There's a marine deck at the stern where we keep the jet skis and power boats.'

'We?' She pounced on this right away. 'Does the owner know you make free with his possessions? I feel I should know who owns the *Black Diamond*. I'm sure I read somewhere that he's a tech billion-aire with royal connections, and a reputation to make your toes curl…' Her thoughtful frown sharpened into an appraising stare. 'So you're no barfly, but a superfit member of the crew on a fabulous yacht. Who might even be able to get me a job on board,' she added with a winning smile.

Luca's mouth tugged slightly. It could have been a smile if his eyes hadn't been so calculating. She knew that feeling. Keeping a resolutely upbeat expression was making her muscles ache, but who wanted to employ a harassed-looking woman?

'Please tell your employer I'll do anything—within reason,' she added quickly. 'If you could arrange a meeting with whoever hires and fires, I won't let you down.'

Relief dashed over her like a great, drowning wave when Luca agreed. Impulsively, she stood on tiptoes to plant a kiss on his chin. Not her best decision, she realised when she saw the look in his eyes. She wasn't playing with fire, she was walking into it. She should be guarding her heart, not giving it away to the first man who offered to do something for her.

His overriding urge was to kiss her back. Which was crazy here in gossip central, aka the lobby of Saint-Tropez's most fashionable watering hole, but Samia's kiss was both a surprise and amazing. She felt so soft and warm against his hard frame, and smelled so good. He wanted nothing more than to kiss away the shadows in her eyes. Her zany sense of humour lifted him, while the sense of desperation he detected behind her jauntiness intrigued him.

'My priority remains finding a job,' she told him bluntly, in case he harboured any amorous notions, he presumed.

'You'd do better in an interview if your stomach isn't growling,' he observed.

'Then, you have my permission to feed me.'

And afterwards? She would join him on board or not. If she did, she would be one hell of a distraction from the ugliness banging in his brain that said he'd let his brother down. The world had judged Pietro a more than worthy heir to the throne of Madlena, while Luca was the spare, the bad boy, the rebellious teen; a dark and mysterious figure who was said to run dangerous missions, and who looked like a pirate, sailed like a pirate and, if the scandal sheets were to be believed, rampaged through countless love affairs like a pirate. He had a lot of work to do before he could convince his people that he was not the devil to Pietro's saint.

Samia and her enormous backpack jostled him as they reached the door.

'Hands off,' she said when he offered to carry it for her. 'I'll have you know that this is a highly prized fashion item.'

'In whose universe?'

'And contains all my worldly goods.'

Why? he wondered. Her green eyes were dancing with laughter, but the shadows were still there. Samia might turn out to be an amusing coda to his trip, or a complete non-event. Either way, he'd board his yacht and sail home.

'There's just one more thing,' she said as the doorman advanced.

'Only one?' He groaned theatrically.

'Any job I take must be lawful and respectable.'

'Of course. What do you take me for?'

'I don't know yet,' she said honestly.

Recognising him, the uniformed doorman flung the door wide. *'Principe!'* he gushed, bowing low. 'What an honour!'

'Principe?' Breath shot from Samia's lungs. *'What?'*

Numb with shock, she stared at Luca, and it took a few moments before the pieces fell into place.

'I do know you… Of course I do. You don't work on the *Black Diamond*. You own it. You're Luca Fortebracci, heir to the throne of Madlena since your brother's tragic—' She stopped when she saw the expression on Luca's face. 'I'm so sorry. That was clumsy of me. I've been off the grid too long, but that's no excuse for not thinking before I open my mouth. How insensitive you must think me.'

'Why should I think that?'

Nice words, but Luca's tone was frighteningly clipped and cold. She braced herself as he continued, 'Are you in a position to offer sympathy? Do you know me? Did you know my brother?'

In the space of a brief few moments, the sexy, laid-back guy she'd met in a bar had changed into a cold and distant prince.

'We need to clear the doorway,' he rapped. 'More diners are arriving.'

Cut him some slack! His grief was still raw, and she'd clearly poured salt on the wounds. 'I'm really sorry. If you'd rather I didn't come with you, I'll just go.'

Luca kept his hold on her arm and then she saw

his need to hurry. *Photographs*. Those who had witnessed the mini drama between them were surreptitiously capturing the moment on their phones.

'Come on,' Luca gritted out. 'Let's get out of here. There's a time and a place, and this isn't it.'

She knew how it felt to be the focus of everyone's interest, and though in her case the scandal had soon passed over, forgotten as someone else came under the spotlight, for royalty it was remorseless.

'I understand your need for discretion,' she told Luca, 'and I get that everything needs to be calm and orderly in the enclosed confines of a yacht, but please don't let this stand in the way of you considering me for a job. I really need something, and I'll keep my head down and work as hard as I can. We've both relaxed more than perhaps we intended to over this past hour or so—equally, I think we both know playtime is over.'

Luca drew to a halt on the pavement outside. Narrowing his eyes, he pierced her with a stare, as if mining for truth, and then, as if he'd come to a decision, he jerked his chin, indicating it was time to move on.

Stay or go? Glancing behind them, she went with the best option.

She'd touched a nerve by mentioning his brother's death, but Luca knew that Samia wasn't responsible for his guilt. If he wanted her on board, he had to ease off. In her favour, having learned he was a prince, and no doubt recalling his colourful reputation, had made no difference to her opinion of him, and there was no doubt she was a welcome change from simpering princesses and spoiled celebrities.

'Hey! *Watch out!*' A surge of concern ripped through him as she almost stepped into the path of a passing coach. 'I get you had a shock back there, but there's no need to throw yourself under a bus.'

She looked at him, weighed him up, and then laughed. 'Wow, I thought I'd lost you there for a moment. Welcome back.'

He huffed something resembling a laugh as he stared down into her heart-shaped face.

'Are you sure this is good enough for your princely self?' she asked as they approached the burger stall.

'On the basis that your mouth will be too full of food for more cheeky remarks, I'd say it's the perfect choice.'

A rebellious glint fired in her eyes that promised more entertainment down the line. What had happened to his much-vaunted control? Wrecked, he concluded when he'd bought the burger and watched Samia lap red sauce from her fingers.

'So what do you think you know about me?' he asked as a distraction from his body's urgent prompting to do more with this woman than eat burgers.

'Very little,' she admitted. 'Only what I've read in the press.'

'You mentioned being off the radar a while. Is that because of this trip?'

She confined her answer to a brief nod.

'I was hoping for more than that,' he admitted.

Flattening her lips, she said nothing, but her eyes told him firmly, *Back off.*

He liked that she stood up to him, but as he caught sight of the *Black Diamond*, apparently floating serenely on a tranquil ocean, when he knew all about dangerous currents lurking beneath, it was as if sailing was a metaphor for life. He didn't know this woman, or the harm she could do to him.

'Don't you want to share?' she asked, holding out the greasy bun.

His mind flew to the galley on board the *Black Diamond* where his Michelin-starred chef would be preparing some delicacy to tempt him. 'Thank you, but I'll pass.'

'Not up to your princely standards?'

He gave her a look, then thought of the unidentifiable sludge he used to eat in the army. 'I have a healthy appetite, and it will take more than a mouthful of meat to satisfy me.'

Her cheeks fired red, but she drove past her embarrassment to assure him she would remember that, if she got a job in his galley.

Or in his bed.

'Once you've had a chance to settle in, I'll assess what you can do.'

'Settle in?' she queried, pulling her head back to frown at him. 'What do you think I've got in this knapsack? It isn't the Tardis. If I have to wear a uniform it would double the number of outfits I own. Will I have to wear a uniform?'

A number of options flashed into his mind. 'Not right away.'

She lightened him, he admitted silently, and no one but his beloved *nonna* could do that. A better state of mind was good for him, and could only be good for his people. Her banter amused him, and her quick wits kept his on point. Either she'd annoy the hell out of him when they were on board, in which case she'd leave at the next port, or she'd join him in bed.

'Will we be sailing straight to Madlena?' she asked as if reading his mind.

'I haven't decided yet,' he said as they approached his private dock.

'Aren't you due at an enthronement in a couple of weeks' time?'

His hackles rose. He didn't need a reminder that the gulf between the freedom he was enjoying now and the shackles he was facing then was closing. 'What's that to you?'

'Hold on to your hat,' she exclaimed. 'I'm just trying to work out your schedule, so I know where I stand.'

His schedule might have to undergo some radical changes if he was to fit in an interlude of pleasure before duty claimed him. That gap had almost closed already, he concluded as they approached the tight security cordon at the entrance to his dock. 'We might take a small diversion.'

'We?' she queried.

'The crew and I.'

The Fortebracci dynasty would have to wait a little longer for its next Prince to forge some cold-blooded alliance with a po-faced princess. Spending time with a woman who gave as good as she got held far more appeal.

CHAPTER FOUR

HER HEAD WAS SPINNING. What had she done? Where was she going? Who was she going with?

Luca was a prince?

The facts kept bouncing around her head, while she went hot and cold, and her heart refused to stop pounding. She tried to act normally, as if she didn't care, but of course she cared. She cared for her safety. She cared for her heart, and Luca definitely provoked a reaction from her. It was impossible to be near him without feeling something. And what would he say when he found out what she did for a living? But she needed this job, and she'd be lying if she said her nose wasn't twitching at the scent of a story. How could two brothers who'd been so close end up with one being dubbed a saint and the other a sinner? Surely, the truth must lie somewhere in between? That Luca was complex, she had no doubt, but was he as bad as he was painted?

'You're having doubts?' he guessed as the guards at the gate saluted and stood back respectfully. 'Now's your chance to change your mind…'

'I'm fine.' Whatever she discovered about Luca, she'd keep it to herself. To broadcast details of his private life would be both intrusive and dishonest. Her heart was safe because he didn't want it, and he'd never find out that she was rubbish in bed, as her ex had insisted, because she had no intention of going there.

'Nothing serious, I hope?' she prompted when she saw that Luca was frowning at a message on his phone.

He hummed and said nothing, but his expression was like a storm approaching, and made her wonder if she was being too hasty in agreeing to this trip.

Once on board, she would untangle her thoughts. Beneath her blasé front she was still reeling from the effects of living with a bully. And yes, she'd been frightened of him…frightened of his power and reach. Divorce had not divided them, as she'd hoped, but had only made him more vindictive. Once on board, she'd be safe from him—for the duration of the voyage, at least. She must make the most of learning how the super-rich lived, and maybe write about it one day in general terms. There was no need to mention Luca specifically.

'Is this where we wait for transport to the yacht?' she asked, gazing around in wonder at the luxuriously appointed seating area, manned by uniformed attendants serving canapés and champagne.

'Not to your liking?' he teased while she trembled. The frisson was all due to him. Luca only had to look at her for her body to yearn for the excitement it had missed. Escaping the past was the light at the end of the tunnel, and she was eager to get there, desperate to march forward into a better future. 'A glass of sparkling water would be great.' Keeping a clear head would be better still.

Luca also refused champagne, saying he would be sailing later.

A pang of disappointment reminded her that a new recruit for the prince's yacht would hardly be at the top of his agenda. Regret still formed like a ball in the pit of her stomach, while Luca paced like a tiger with a thorn in its pad. They were both eager to get on board, but for different reasons. She might be hungry to continue the getting-to-know-you process, but he was returning to an activity he loved, and an unimaginably privileged lifestyle that defined him. *Grow up. Get real.* If she was lucky she might get that job, and occasionally see him in passing.

But she couldn't help herself. She never could. Her mother used to say she was born asking questions. 'So… Madlena?' she prompted.

'I'll answer questions when we're on board.'

Luca's tone was clipped, as if to discourage all further conversation. She couldn't blame him. He was a prince.

A prince in mourning.

He owned the yacht.

And soon his freedom to sail will be cut short.

At best, she'd be a lowly member of crew.

But I could still help him.

And how exactly would she do that?

I'll find a way.

'And when we're on board you'll ask no questions.'

She pulled back her head with surprise, then remembered he'd been hounded by the press, and must have had his fill of questions. When news of his brother's death broke, press opinion had been heavily weighted against the Pirate Prince taking over from Prince Pietro, who had never been known to put a foot wrong. Even she had to admit it would take something special to restore his reputation. Could she help him do that? Almost certainly not. Any influence she might have had in the press had gone down the tubes on the day she'd agreed to marry the newspaper mogul who owned the paper she wrote for. He'd used every threat in the book to make her change her words for his, and after her mother's suicide, when she'd thought it couldn't get any worse, his threat to ruin her father's life had proved her wrong. She would have done anything to save her father from more grief, and she had.

'You'll need to take those boots off when you board.'

'Of course I will.' She could have kissed Luca for giving her something so straightforward to think about. He'd stopped pacing, and was standing close enough to touch. Their hands were almost brushing against each other, and hers were tingling, as was her thigh closest to his. Luca was so overwhelmingly masculine, her body was acutely aware of him. The power he exuded was very different from that of her ex, but he'd been a bully, while Luca offered choices. Sex with her ex had been brutal and fast, which had resulted in Samia dreading the act, while Luca, for all his rampant masculinity, only filled her with the yearning to be touched with tenderness and skill.

Maybe there was hope for her yet, she reflected wryly as Luca, having noticed her interest, stared keenly at her. Not *much* hope, she concluded, remembering she was about to step into the unknown with a man she hardly knew.

'At last,' he announced as a sleek black powerboat cruised to the side of the dock.

Taking a risk had surely never felt this good. She was excited. And why not? A threadbare, penniless nomad, without a job or a home to go to, and a past so bleak it threatened to swamp her, was on her way to a billionaire's yacht.

As Luca went to help his men, she took the chance, while ropes were secured and fenders tossed over the side to prevent the hull scraping against the dock, to do some research on her phone. What she discovered about Prince Luca Fortebracci only made her hungry to learn more. The Pirate Prince had quite a history. Where romance was concerned, he appeared to be a generous lover, yet had never formed a lasting attachment. An entrepreneur almost by accident, who'd started his global business in his bedroom as a boy, whatever was written about him in the press—or whatever Luca thought about himself—he was considered a national hero in Madlena, so why was he so tense going home? For all his wealth and success, he seemed a solitary figure, apart from the beloved grandmother he so often quoted in the press.

'Ready?' he prompted.

Any minute now, she would be stepping from her world into his, so it was time to pull herself together, get ready to embrace whatever came next.

Don't get ahead of yourself, her nitpicky inner voice warned. *If you're lucky, you might get a job on the* Black Diamond *where Luca will most certainly be your boss, and so high above your lowly status you might not see him again. This is a chance to escape the shadow of your ex and plan the rest of your life, and that's all it is.*

And do a bit more research about Luca, surely— to satisfy her curiosity, if nothing else. Supposing her inner voice was right about not seeing much of Luca once they were on board, surely with her history in the bedroom she should be relieved. Anything more than a business relationship came with its own set of complications.

Shouldn't I, of all people, be wary of powerful men?

Turning for one last look around the shore, she saw so many things to reassure her—children playing, families sipping drinks—and yet the rope was playing out and soon she'd be leaving those familiar scenes far behind.

'I'll put a boat at your disposal if you change your mind once we're on board.'

Could he read her mind? Her anxiety must be showing.

'You'll have full Wi-Fi access,' Luca continued smoothly, as a boarding ramp was secured between the quay and the powerboat. 'If you lose signal, we have satellite phones. Why don't you ring your parents now to reassure them?'

'My mother's dead.' She clapped a hand across her mouth. The words had shot out before she could stop them. 'I'm so sorry. You must think me thoughtless mentioning something like that.'

'Why would I? I'm sorry for your loss.'

But he was frowning. 'And I for yours,' she said. Luca's face had grown closed and unreadable again. They had both experienced tragedy, and were both struggling to reclaim some semblance of normality in lives that suddenly made very little sense. The press had disclosed hardly anything about Prince Pietro's death, beyond describing it as 'a freak accident,' which was enough to rouse the curiosity of any investigative journalist, even one supposedly taking a lengthy sabbatical.

'How did your mother die?'

The shock of the question jolted her back to the present, and she decided to be equally blunt. 'She took her own life.' Rather than face the shame of Samia's father being brought before a judge. The guilt that hit was familiar. Could she have done more to save her mother? And now it was followed by a second thought: Did Luca have a similar demon to wrestle?

'We both have reason to grieve,' he observed in a clipped tone.

'And to go forward.' Every day she renewed her determination to return to the work she loved. Her fall from grace had been spectacular. One day her column was praised to the skies for its brave exposure of criminals, and the next, when her writing had inexplicably changed, from seeing both sides of an argument to only one, that of her ex, her readers had deserted her in droves. When she'd threatened to make his deception public, he'd promised she'd never work again, and when they'd divorced, he'd vowed to pursue her to the ends of the earth. That was why she'd left London with just the clothes on her back, and her mother's old hiking boots to keep her grounded. She needed space from evil to stand a chance of climbing back.

'Hang on. Sit down,' Luca said as he escorted her onto the powerboat.

Whatever they knew or didn't know about each other, Luca remained a comforting presence at her side as she took her place at the prow of the boat. To begin with, it was a comfortable ride—the skipper kept strictly to the speed limits—but once they were out at sea and the harbour police were left behind, he opened up the engines and the prow rose out of the water.

They hit a wake. She yelped and bounced onto Luca, who held her firmly, keeping her safe. Close contact was electrifying. He felt so warm, so strong like a rock. His hands were roughened by sailing, but that was another point in his favour. She was done with hands mauling her that had never done an honest day's work. Far from saving her father when she married her ex, she'd only made matters worse, given him more cause to threaten and bully her. She could only think now that she'd been reeling with grief after the death of her mother. Her father was weak and deep in debt, and she'd had to do something to save him. Her ex would keep him out of prison, he'd promised. Well, that had gone well. Her father was still in jail.

She noticed Luca was looking thoughtful as he read another text on his phone. Trouble? Could she help? She didn't know him well enough to ask. Did she care for him so much already? Was it even possible for that depth of connection to be instant? Had she already forgotten she had promised herself she'd guard her heart?

Enjoy the moment for what it is, her inner voice advised, *and stop worrying about what might happen, let alone what happened in the past. Live for now or you'll regret it.*

Turning her face to the sun, she smiled as the roar of the engines confirmed the distance they were travelling, from the mainland out to sea. It was as if she were flying across the ocean with a strong man at her back. How hard was it to be optimistic?

'This is amazing!' she called out, beginning to understand Luca's passion for sailing. Blue sky and a silver sea bathed in sunlight were nothing short of spectacular. The air was as pure as a new page waiting to be written on. 'I can't thank you enough for giving me this opportunity.'

'You'll have to work hard,' Luca warned.

'I'm ready.'

Was that a flash of calculation in his eyes? She didn't remain anxious for long. It wasn't possible with heat rippling through her veins like hot chocolate on a cold afternoon just from being close to Luca. Maybe she should be asking what jobs were available on board, but why spoil the moment when she felt properly alive for the first time in ages? Luca had reminded her how exciting it could be to pit her wits against an intelligent opponent, and offer opinions without constantly being mocked. She couldn't remember the last time she'd felt like this.

It was as if he'd read her thoughts. Taking hold of her hand, he stared at the mark left by her wedding ring. Removing her hand, she levelled a stare on his face. 'You must be wondering why I'm here. I know I am,' she admitted.

'You're escaping,' he said.

'Perhaps we both are.' She noticed he didn't deny it.

'Why are you so down on yourself?' he asked Samia. Beauty was so often marred by high self-esteem, but Samia was completely unspoiled. More of her bright copper hair had escaped her careless updo, while exposure to sunshine and wind from the sea had pinked up her face, adding to the sprinkling of freckles on her nose. She was lovely, and should be full of confidence.

'I'm not down on myself, but you're a prince and a billionaire, and I'm no one,' she said, 'so why take an interest in me?'

'*No one?* Did your ex tell you that?' He shook his head with contempt. 'Everyone's someone, and deserving of equal consideration.'

'In an ideal world, maybe,' Samia agreed with a rueful laugh. 'But not everyone's *someone* to the same degree you are.'

'If you're talking wealth and titles—' he spread his arms wide '—an accident of birth doesn't make me better than anyone else. Money? It depends what you do with it, but it's no guarantee of happiness. It doesn't make the bad times easier to bear.'

'I'm sorry.' She touched his arm sympathetically. 'I hardly know you, but your loss is so keen I can feel it.'

He blanked the comment. Unburdening himself to a stranger wasn't his way. What would it change? Nothing.

'I'm sorry, you must think me intrusive,' she added quickly, 'but if I can help in any way—'

'You can't,' he said flatly.

As the powerboat slowed beneath the shadow of Luca's yacht, Samia gazed up towards the yawning entrance that gaped blankly in its side. Borders she'd crossed had never intimidated her as much as this one, but she was determined not to show it as Luca stood. He was quite distant now, though still polite. Was that, as she had suspected, a sign of things to come? Employee and boss. Prince and civilian. The grief of losing his brother was shut away somewhere so deep she couldn't touch it. However strong an attraction she felt, they were strangers, and seemed destined to remain so. That didn't stop her feeling sorry for him, and wishing she could help. Luca might wield the power of a Caesar, but like everyone else on the face of the earth, when it came down to it, he was on his own.

He crossed the gap between the rolling powerboat and the comparatively stable yacht in one stride, and waited on the other side to steady her. His firm touch on her wrist was reassuring. Luca didn't frighten her like her ex, and it was a relief to discover she could still feel warmth, and be attracted to a man, and that—for her, at least—no amount of mistreatment could completely frighten off Mother Nature.

'Welcome on board,' he said as she leapt across the foaming gulf. 'I hope you find the experience worthwhile.'

'I'm sure I shall,' she said, matching him for politeness. She was eager to sample all the new things on board, and looking forward to meeting his crew.

The crew gave her a warmer welcome than she'd expected. Shaking hands firmly with each of them, she decided that she would like it here, with or without Luca's involvement. *Though with would be better*, she reflected as he touched her arm to move her on.

CHAPTER FIVE

THE EMAIL HE read on the powerboat was from the excellent team he had working for him. For now, the information they had on Samia Smith was enough for him. As requested, the answers to his questions appeared in bullet points, which they would send him a further list of soon.

A wife would go a long way to settling the distress in Madlena following Prince Pietro's death.

News of Prince Luca's marriage would silence the naysayers, proving intentions towards Madlena are both serious and long-term.

Arriving with a bride, followed by a formal blessing in the cathedral for everyone to enjoy, has been received with unanimous approval.

Good. It was his intention that the Pirate Prince would be seen as a man determined to change. At some point in the future, when confidence in his reign was fully restored, his wife could be discreetly let go with his blessing and thanks, together with a healthy pension for life. Any children, if there were any, would stay with him. There would be no repeat of his brother's misstep.

The magic of a royal wedding never fails...

A rather cynical take, to be sure, but he would not deny the citizens of Madlena the reassurance they so badly needed. His life no longer belonged to him, but to his people, who only knew him through his army career, and lurid rumours in the press. Trust took time. He accepted that, but an intelligent, lively bride he already found attractive was a good, solid start. He'd inform Samia that he intended to marry her when the time was right. She was the perfect solution to his dilemma. The fact this had happened so fast was no reason to doubt his decision. He would soon make her see the benefits of becoming his wife.

He skim read the rest of the email, which rambled on about plans for a wedding to a woman he hadn't proposed to yet. A detailed agenda for the ceremony would be found in the Red Box, together with a full CV of the woman he had asked his team to investigate.

If Your Serene Highness has an opportunity to review the biographies and photographs of the various suitable princesses that we've also included and let us know your decision, we'll move things along

quickly and have your choice of bride delivered to
the yacht for your perusal forthwith.

Forthwith? He curbed a smile as he glanced at
Samia, wondering if any of these same advisors
would have the courage to inform Samia she had
been *delivered* to his yacht for perusal by the prince.
The solution to Madlena's woes lay in his hands,
not in a document contained in the Red Box, listing
'suitable' princesses.

He texted while Samia was taking everything in.

No princesses. I already have someone in mind.

Why waste time on unknown quantities when
a challenging prospect was standing right in front
of him?

Out of the frying pan, into the fire? Samia wondered
as she gazed around.

She had never been anywhere like the deck of
the *Black Diamond*. It was so vast, so clean and so
very high-tech. Which she should have accepted, as
it belonged to a tech billionaire who just happened
to be a prince. Everything had gone so smoothly…
Too smoothly? she wondered as Luca ushered her
on. Did he have an agenda behind his generous invitation? There was no mention of a job yet, or even
an interview.

Tell me I haven't blundered into trouble again!
She needed reassurance, and doubted she would

get it. Luca would most likely go about his duties and forget she was around. Stiffening her resolve, she decided to talk to him while she could. Exploring the *Black Diamond* would have to wait.

He was issuing instructions to some members of the crew. 'Excuse my interruption,' she said politely, 'but I wonder if you could introduce me to your purser?'

The crew dispersed at a nod from Luca.

'Or whoever interviews candidates for jobs on board, please.'

'You're already hired,' he said.

'For what position?'

'Jack of all trades. Whatever you're called upon to do.'

'I need more than that. I need specifics.'

'Not now,' he stated firmly.

She was a grown woman with a phone and the ability to call for help if she needed to. She told herself to calm down and look at this sensibly. Having got herself into this situation, she could either see it through, or take a boat back to shore as Luca had already suggested. His crew respected him, and appeared glad to have him back. There were no funny looks, or anything to make her feel nervous. She could get to know him on board, and understand this incredible lifestyle.

'When?' she asked, softening the question with a smile.

'After dinner,' he suggested. 'Why are you still trembling?' he asked, frowning.

Was it that obvious? It was the Luca effect, but she wasn't going to tell him that. 'The breeze is kicking up,' she excused. 'Time to go below decks to my quarters?' She couldn't drop a hint any bigger than that.

'This is a sailing yacht,' he reminded her, 'and not one of those "floating office blocks" you referred to.'

'And it's lovely,' she said.

The quirk of one ebony brow warned her not to play with fire. No danger of that. She doubted she'd be on board long enough to get her fingers burned.

Samia remained uncharacteristically silent, which threw him. Inviting a woman onto his yacht within an hour of meeting her was not normal behaviour. The text from his team had endorsed his belief that a mix of gut instinct and feral lust could occasionally provide a solution to a problem. His next task was to convince Samia to become his bride.

Well, that should be easy, he mused dryly, taking in the stubborn set of her chin. Samia owed Madlena nothing, and him even less, and, while many might jump at the chance of marrying a prince, he doubted Samia would be the least bit impressed by either status or wealth. Independent and feisty, she would determine her own route through life. It was his task to make sure that route led to him.

In pursuit of a seemingly ideal solution, he ran a list of benefits due a royal bride through his mind: the throne of Madlena, priceless crown jewels, front row seats at every prestige event, private jets, super-yachts, palaces and homes across the world. Syco-phants aplenty. He grimaced at this last thought. *Must try harder*, he reflected with a tinge of amuse-ment as Samia glanced his way. It was hard not to be captivated by her enthusiasm as he took her on a tour of the yacht. How long was it since he'd witnessed such innocent pleasure, or that one of the many visi-tors to the yacht had dared to admit that anything excited them? It was cool to be blasé, something that seemed to have passed Samia by. She liked some-thing, or she didn't, and she wasn't afraid to tell him, whether her opinion was *cool* or not.

'Teams of stylists must have worked on this for months,' she said as they crossed the grand salon.

'Years in the planning,' he revealed, amused to discover she was padding alongside him barefoot. But of course, she didn't have anything with her, he remembered, apart from a few oddments in her backpack. All that was about to change.

'It's a bit bland for me,' she admitted as glass doors slid open at their approach.

'Bland?' he queried, a little taken aback.

'All this white and taupe is a bit dated, don't you think? I like a splash of colour.'

'On board my black yacht?' he suggested with amusement.

'Why not?' she enthused.

Similar to the modern art in his quarters on board, he was thinking. He'd never noticed the rest of the décor before, but seeing it through Samia's eyes gave it a new slant. As she took a closer look at a maritime map on the wall, his thoughts grew to encompass her soft skin beneath his hands, and the supple warmth of her body straining beneath his. The enticing scent of wildflowers and heat floated in her wake, and for the first time he could remember, he was stirred on board his yacht to do more than haul sail.

'First impressions?' he demanded.

'You are the master of all you survey,' Samia declared, 'and the *Black Diamond* is a billionaire's plaything.'

'It's a serious sailing yacht, not some toy.'

'You asked for my opinion.'

And unfortunately that was what she'd given him, straight up with no frills. 'Why don't you write a report?' he asked cynically.

'If that's what you'd like?'

She'd taken him seriously, and he couldn't bring himself to mock this straightforward woman. 'I would,' he said. What harm could it do?

'I've spent too long keeping my mouth shut in the past,' she explained. 'I've no intention of making that mistake again, so what I see is what I say, and if you'd like me to write it down, I'm happy to do so.'

'It's a deal,' he agreed. This microfact made him hungry to hear more. There was nothing he liked better than a challenge, and Samia would not agree with him simply to garner praise. This made her a refreshing change, and the perfect choice of bride for him. But he wasn't going to let her off too lightly.

'No wonder sailing is my passion,' he said dryly.

'Because the yacht doesn't answer back?' she suggested.

'Do I need a better reason?' From the blackest of moods earlier in the day, she'd lifted him, and it was a relief to discover he could still tap into feelings.

'I thought you were going to show me to my quarters?' she prompted. 'I sure as hell won't find them by myself. All this for one man,' she breathed in awe as they walked on.

'And one opinionated woman,' he added with an amused sideways look. 'I think most people would sympathise and say I badly need space between us.'

'Most people would sympathise with me, I think you'll find,' she countered with a cheeky smile.

He had the satisfaction of hearing her gasp when he opened a door leading into the burnished wood-panelled entrance to the suite of rooms he had chosen for Samia. 'This is more like it,' she exclaimed. 'Forget bland. I can't imagine anything more beautiful than this.'

'All my brother's design.' The words came out awkwardly, clipped and emotion-free. He still found it hard to talk about Pietro and this suite had been his brother's vision for guests on board the *Black Diamond*.

Guests? Luca remembered asking Pietro. *But this is a sailing boat.*

And you should not be such a loner, Pietro had insisted. *It's not good for you, Luca...*

In Pietro's trademark style, everything in the suite Luca had chosen for Samia was lavish and

flamboyant. There were jewel-coloured rugs beneath their feet, and intricate hangings on the wall
above a vast, canopied bed that was almost a joke
out at sea. Only the most exclusive and vivid fabrics had been used for soft furnishings, and to dress
the windows… Silks, satin, velvet and chiffon, the
latter billowing lazily in the sea breeze blowing in
from the balcony. Acres of lovingly polished wood
and brass complemented these lavish adornments,
and the setting was further enhanced by paintings
of sailing ships through the ages, and good-looking
men in a variety of impeccable uniforms.

'Your brother had great taste,' Samia commented
as she trailed her fingertips across the arm of a comfortable chair lavishly upholstered in a luxurious
velvet tapestry.

'He was a great one for history, and for design.
Pietro could have had a great future ahead of him,
had he not been a prince.'

'But surely, being a prince *is* a great future?'

'Not for Pietro.' The words were wrenched out
of him and each left a jagged wound. 'Pietro always
preferred a quiet life, out of the limelight. He enjoyed
designing sets,' he reminisced, thinking back to the
childhood concerts Pietro had enjoyed putting on.
'A quiet life was the only thing my brother craved,
but that was not to be…'

Dragging his thoughts out of the past, he took
a look around the suite again. It was every bit as
grand and impressive as Samia thought it, though in
his opinion the décor belonged in a museum, rather

than a state-of-the-art sailing yacht that had been built to Luca's design. But he and his brother had always enjoyed doing things together, and he had wanted Pietro to be part of this too... *Dio!* How he missed him.

'You okay?' Samia asked.

'My brother was never a sailor,' he explained, clinging to cold, hard facts. 'Design was his strength and his passion.'

'At which he excelled,' Samia said frankly. 'He had wonderful taste.'

Her tone was quiet and understanding, and lacked pity, which was more important, as it allowed him to say without betraying any emotion, 'He was a wonderful man.'

'And you loved him, as I'm sure Prince Pietro loved you.'

Where had she sprung from, this woman fate had placed in his way? When he looked at her, he thought back to previous guests with their artfully tousled hair and intricate make-up, bringing on board cabin trunks bulging with clothes, only to discover that nothing they'd brought with them was remotely suitable for a sailing yacht. Naturally, they ordered more at his expense, prompting deliveries from Paris, Rome and Milan to arrive at ports ahead of them. Much of this forgotten inventory still hung in protective covers in Samia's dressing room.

'There's a swimming pool on board. Two, in fact,' he revealed. 'Feel free to use them.'

'There's one for your crew?'

'There are two pools you can use.'

'Wonderful…but I don't have a costume with me.'

'You'll find some in your dressing room that have never been worn. Help yourself. At least one of them should fit.'

'I'm not sure I'll be swimming.'

Who could blame her for not being thrilled at the thought of wearing a previous guest's clothes? 'The costumes are brand new,' he explained. 'Don't let pride get in your way. Consider anything you find in the dressing room a down payment for whatever job I decide you'll do.'

'I'd rather be paid a wage, if that's all right. I'm not very good at taking handouts.'

'So I remember,' he said, remembering the ten-euro note she'd insisted on giving him for the hamburger and the water. 'How about I pay you a wage too?'

She shrugged and smiled a crooked smile. 'It might be possible to come to an accommodation.'

When Samia looked like that, she was irresistible. 'Make use of any of the clothes you find in the dressing room. You'd be doing me a favour. All they represent to me at the moment is money down the drain.'

It was hard not to imagine her in one of the many evening gowns. How Samia would feel about that, though, was another matter. Most of them were extremely revealing, and she didn't move in the same brittle circles he did, packed with career courtesans making it their life's work to date rich, successful men in order to piggyback on their privileged lifestyles. Putting their wares on display in the full expectation of having them decorated with precious gems was all part of the game.

'I can wear anything I find?' she exclaimed with what appeared to be genuine excitement. 'Does that go for all your crew?'

He gave her a look that shut her up.

'Anyway, you're very generous,' she added. 'I always liked to play dress-up as a child, though that involved a thousand different ways with a tablecloth and things I borrowed from my mother's wardrobe.'

Seeing her grow wistful, he was more determined than ever to read the report on her that his team had sent over.

'Sorry if I'm holding you up,' she added as he turned for the door.

'You're not, or I wouldn't be here,' he said bluntly. The more he learned about this fascinating woman, the more certain he became that he'd made a good choice of bride. Samia would always be her own person, but he admired that. Her natural friendliness had already quickly endeared her to his crew, and vanity had no place in her life. His people would love that. She hadn't touched her hair once since they'd met, or fixed her lip gloss—if she was even wearing any. Understated, with personality to spare, she'd already proved she was kind and thoughtful, and the citizens of Madlena were hungry for a personal touch after his brother's shyness, which had manifested itself as apparent aloofness. She was funny and quirky, and who didn't like that? When he returned to Madlena, everything would be for the benefit of his people, and not for how it made him look. This *was* a politically astute marriage, just not the sort his people probably anticipated. How better to reassure the citizens of Madlena than to introduce them to his down-to-earth bride?

How can I be so sure she's so right for the role when I hardly know her?

With a full report waiting on his desk in the Red Box, knowing everything about Samia was only a matter of time.

'Where's your accommodation?' she asked out of interest when Luca turned to leave the suite his brother had designed.

'Down the corridor from yours, so if you need anything—'

'I won't,' she said quickly from a mouth turned dry. 'Surely, I won't really be staying here?' She stared around the elaborate room. First the clothes, and now this fabulous suite of rooms? Why wasn't she to wear the simple black rig all the crew wore, and stay in crew quarters? 'If you tell me where the crew sleeps, I'll be happy to find my way there.'

'You're staying here,' he insisted flatly.

'What?'

'Pietro designed this area to be used.'

'So I'm just filling a slot?' She felt relieved.

Luca shrugged his magnificent shoulders. 'Yes, you'll actually be doing me a favour if you stay here, as there's no more room in the crew area right now.'

'Then…thank you.'

'And as I said about the clothes, you'll be doing me a favour wearing those too.'

Lots of favours, she thought. Would there be a price to pay eventually?

'Freshen up, take a shower and relax while you can,' he recommended.

While you can? What did that mean, exactly?

A frisson of excitement feathered across her skin. It would be churlish to refuse, she decided.

'Last chance to return to shore,' he added, then paused with his hand on the door handle. His lips pressed down. 'Too late.'

Hearing the unmistakeable grind of an anchor being raised, she couldn't keep the panic from her voice as she admitted, 'I didn't realise we were so close to sailing.'

'I made no secret of the fact that I needed to leave,' Luca said levelly.

'No, indeed—it's just that...' Plain and simple? She thought she'd have more time.

'Doubts, Samia? Better say so now.'

'No.'

'I can still get you back to shore in one of the small crafts we keep on board.'

'That won't be necessary, but thank you.' She'd made her decision and she wasn't backing down now, but what exactly had she agreed to...? Work as yet unspecified, and a suite of rooms fit for a princess located handily next to those of a prince. Was she really so naïve? Luca had shown little sign of wanting to romance her... Yes. She was that naïve.

Was the Pirate Prince noted for his romantic nature, or was his calculating sexuality all he expected it to take to achieve another conquest?

She didn't have to do anything she didn't want to do. One thing she was certain of about Luca was that he didn't have to force himself on a woman, or mistreat her, or mock her, or do any of the things that she'd thought had put her off men for good.

'So you're happy to stay on board?' he asked.

Gathering herself, she confirmed this. 'If you'll still have me, but I do insist on making myself useful. Or how else can I pay for my passage?'

To his credit, Luca didn't say anything to alarm her, though his mouth did tug up a fraction at one corner. 'I'm sure we can find something for you to do,' he said as he opened the door. 'But for now I'm going to leave you to take that shower, which will give me a chance to decide exactly what to do with you.'

She got the distinct impression from his expression that her fate was already decided, but instead of alarm bells ringing, as they surely should have done, she felt incredibly excited by the prospect of whatever lay ahead.

CHAPTER SIX

HE DIDN'T RETURN to his suite right away, or even to his study where the Red Box was waiting. Instead, he retraced his steps to the grand salon to take a proper look at the space through Samia's eyes. And, following her verdict, it did strike him as insipid.

Nothing would ever be boring with Samia.

His yacht was state-of-the-art fierce, while this reception area was like a tepid bath, neither ice nor fire. And he craved fire, he thought, brooding on a pair of emerald eyes.

What is this grand salon used for? she must have wondered. Grand dinner parties where equally grand food and drink were served to grand guests.

He could almost hear Samia observing, *No invitation for me, then...?*

Those grand guests would all glut themselves at his expense. No one had ever been known to refuse an invitation from the notorious Pirate Prince, let alone offer the slightest criticism, or an opinion that might differ from his.

He'd rather eat a hamburger with Samia any day of the week.

* * *

She could hardly believe she was soaking in a king-sized tub in a pink veined-marble bathroom the same size as her bedroom at home, bathed in warmth and cloaked in shimmering, rainbow-hued bubbles. This was all incredible and new and fabulous—and it wouldn't do to get used to it.

What would it be like to live like this every day? Idle? Great to dream about, but a bit boring to indulge in all the time, though it did take her back to playing make-believe with her mother. Her father had gambled away their money, and her mother, a renowned beauty in her time, had been ill-equipped to deal with the harsh realities of everyday life. Samia had adapted quickly, because she was young and not used to much luxury, as that was reserved for her parents. She hadn't been very old when she'd started to see the cracks beneath the façade of their wealth— maybe six or seven. An empty larder, and holes in the soles of her father's expensive shoes, had told their own story. To begin with, her mother had made the best of things by acting out scenes she would have inhabited at one time, introducing Samia to a glittering world she could only dream about...*before now*.

How her mother would have loved this, she reflected as she trailed her fingertips through the bubbles and swished the warm water. Pressing her lips together hard, she remembered her mother's last note, begging for forgiveness, and saying Samia would be better off without her. Samia only wished they could have talked things through.

Closing her eyes, she sank back with a sigh. Things were rarely what they seemed. Even this incredible encounter with Luca might not be as straightforward as it appeared. More soldier than prince, he could play the role of laid-back charmer equally well. He'd set the restaurant alight with more than a title, good looks, or even his formidable reputation. It was the dangerously glittering glamour he radiated that meant that even when he was barefoot and casually dressed, he drew everyone's eye.

Luca was a powerhouse in every way, though strangely, in spite of her past bad experience, she didn't feel threatened by him. Quite the opposite. He made her feel safe, which only made her all the more determined to help him recover from his brother's death. If she got the chance. Sometimes it was easier for a stranger to see things clearly, and she felt sure that what the people of Madlena needed was a strong prince to lead them forward into a bright and promising future. If Luca remained locked in the past he wouldn't help anyone.

Take that as a lesson for yourself, she concluded. And how exactly could she help Luca, with no job, no home to go to, and a vindictive ex-husband? Looking back, it was obvious her ex had married her for two things: her column and some land in Scotland her father owned, that he had hoped to farm one day. Her ex had said the land shouldn't be farmed as it would make an excellent golf course. She should never have married him, but had run out of options when it came to helping her parents. And he'd seemed so kind at first, paying off her father's debts, and buying her mother some lovely new clothes. It was only later, in one of his drunken rages, that he'd admitted that Samia was incidental to his goal, and if she didn't allow him to edit her work, her father would suffer. When she'd fought back in print, he'd accused her father of fraud, and mysterious funds had started appearing in her father's bank account. When her mother had discovered that the money she had so enjoyed spending was a trap, she'd rapidly gone downhill, while Samia's bewildered father had barely put up a defence at his trial.

Oh, yes, she was perfect princess material, Samia reflected with irony as she climbed out of the bath and grabbed a towel. While Luca was no longer a hot guy lounging in a bar, someone to chat to and spend time with, but master of this ship and a ruler returning to his country. Gaining in princely command with every passing moment. It was hard to see where she fitted into his plans.

Her stomach chose that moment to growl, which brought her down to earth with a bump. She couldn't wait until supper. She was hungry, despite the burger she'd eaten earlier. What were the chances of finding a light snack in the *Black Diamond*'s galley?

There was only one way to find out.

She was determined to remain upbeat, her intention being to quickly ransack the dressing room, find something suitable to wear, and go exploring to find the galley, but when she opened the first drawer and discovered a treasure trove of make-up, she couldn't bring herself to rush. It was as if someone had ordered a high-end cosmetic company's complete range, most of which was still in cellophane-wrapped boxes. This was dress-up with a rocket boost.

After that first discovery, it became a 'no holds barred' trolley dash through every cupboard and drawer. Scarves, purses, costume jewellery and handbags galore were soon scattered about—and how many swimsuits did one person need? Holding up a slinky turquoise number, she realised that whoever had ordered the clothes was about the same size she was. The wardrobes revealed another cache of riches, outfits and evening gowns of a quality she could never afford. Trailing her fingertips across the überdeluxe fabrics, she could only marvel that so many beautiful things had been discarded. Catching sight of herself in the mirror, she laughed. Still wrapped in a towel with her hair all over the place, she looked a sight. 'I am not worthy,' she murmured. But she could wear a cotton sundress...

Right at the back of the wardrobe, she had found a box packed to the brim with a selection of colourful summer dresses. Now it was just a case of deciding which one to wear...

She picked out the plainest frock. It was lovely, actually... Must have slipped through the style police's net: a bright cornflower blue with shoestring straps that tied on the shoulders. The colour matched her optimistic mood, while the dress showed enough of her body without revealing too much. Brushing her hair out until it resembled a fiery cloud, she added a touch of lip gloss and a good lashing of mascara. Why not? This was the first time in a long time she'd felt remotely feminine, or had access to such things. She couldn't do much about her freckles without a bucket of foundation, and she'd have to go barefoot, because none of the sandals she found were either comfortable, or suitable for walking on the deck of a sailing yacht.

Ready!

Staring at herself in the mirror, she wondered how the evening would end. The possibilities were endless—or they might have been, had she been a different person.

Which was the cue for her cheeks to heat up at the thought of Luca touching her…kissing her…

Enough of that! She had a job to do. He must find her one. He had to.

Picking up her notebook, she hugged it close to her chest, but then her grip softened and moved a little, as she began to imagine Luca mapping her breasts, and Luca teasing her promiscuously erect nipples.

Why was her body so eager to lead her into trouble?

Moving on down her ribcage and over her belly, she stopped when she reached the place where his knowing caresses could create a whole world of trouble. Leaving there reluctantly, she trailed her fingertips over thighs tingling just from thinking about him, and went on to rest her hands in the sway of her back, before allowing them to slip even lower to cup her buttocks.

Closing her eyes, she eased back her neck, as certain as she could be that nothing could compare to Luca's touch. Unfortunately, she was equally certain that she'd never find out.

So why not call a halt to all this unnecessary torment? Stop fantasising. Get real!

Not if she had a single functioning brain cell left. Who wanted tepid, when they could have excitement and fire?

Well, that was all well and good, but first she had to exit her make-believe life, and enter the real world where fingers got burned, and excitement could so easily lead to heartache.

A member of the crew dressed all in crisp black directed Samia to the galley. Air-conditioned to a comfortable temperature, the gleaming steel and white space was pristine. A man was lounging against the wall by the cooking station, chatting easily to a chef in whites. A big man. A big hunk of Pirate Prince, looking every bit as dangerous as his sobriquet suggested. He seemed unaware that she'd entered the room.

Wrong.

Luca knew the moment she walked in. 'Welcome,' he said, turning to look at her with a questioning smile. 'Hungry too?'

'One hamburger didn't fill the gap,' she admitted. 'Do you mind if I join you?'

'Not at all.' He scanned her from head to toe, his sharp gaze missing nothing. From his expression, she guessed she looked okay.

'Another hamburger?' he suggested with the hint of a smile that set her heart racing.

'If you just direct me to what I'm allowed to have, I'll sort it out myself,' she said, including the chef. 'I don't want to put you to any trouble. I hope you don't mind me invading your galley?'

My galley, Luca's black stare stated clearly. Pulling away from the wall, he positioned himself between Samia and the handsome young chef.

'I suggest something light,' Luca said, adding, 'and then we'll meet later for a formal dinner on deck.'

'Which will give me a chance to discuss what my job's going to be,' she agreed brightly.

Luca's expression suggested this was not part of his plan.

'Shall I dress for dinner?' she enquired, remaining determinedly upbeat, on the basis that no one wanted to hire a misery.

Luca's hard mouth pressed down and he shrugged. 'I imagine you'd like that.'

She would, but all the gowns she'd found in her dressing room were too sexy, and would put far more of her on show than she was used to. She'd face that problem later, she decided. 'Why don't I prepare something for us to eat?' she suggested. 'Give your chef some time off?'

A flash of something in Luca's eyes said, *This is my galley. This is my crew. Hands off.* Undaunted, she went to wash her hands, and by the time she turned around he'd dismissed the chef. 'I really do need to start paying for my passage,' she explained. 'I'll feel happier if I'm doing something.'

His shrug was one of acquiescence.

'How about pancakes?'

'You're hired,' he laughed.

Her eyes sparkled. 'Then move out of my way.'

Luca watched as she cooked, and then they ate their way through a stack of pancakes with lashings of sugar and lemon, eating at the counter, each with a bottle of beer. Conversation flowed easily, far more easily than she'd imagined, until finally Luca pushed his plate away. 'I'll see you later,' he said as she cleared up, determined to prove herself worthy of being hired.

They settled on meeting again at eight o'clock that evening. 'For dinner beneath a starlit sky,' as he put it with considerable irony.

Who said romance was dead? she reflected with amusement, allowing no emotion to show on her face. But then he did something she had not expected. Reaching across the counter, he brushed some sugar from her lips with the tip of his forefinger, staring into her eyes as he did so. To say her body gave an atomic reaction was probably understating the case. She remained motionless until he stood back, by which time she'd gathered herself enough to say, 'I'll be ready at eight. As will my report.'

'Your report?' he queried, turning on his way to the door.

Her mouth dried. He looked magnificent, such a dark, brooding presence in the steel and white space that she could hardly breathe. 'The report we agreed on? My thoughts on the décor?' she prompted.

He'd been humouring her, she guessed. It was easy to see why Luca had never formed any lasting attachments.

'Your only task tonight,' he informed her, 'is to turn up for dinner at eight o'clock sharp.'

'I'm looking forward to it,' she said mildly, determined not to sacrifice the chance of a job on the altar of her pride. This might be Luca's galley, his yacht and his crew, but she would work her passage, and never bow her head to a man again.

Samia Smith was turning his life upside down. There was such warmth and humour in her eyes, it was hard to resist, but there was also strength and challenge, and that threatened to drive him crazy. Perhaps he'd been spoiled long enough, and it was time to accept that human contact was what he'd been missing. Once he got over his affront, he could see that contact with someone who made no allowance for him being royal was welcome, and much needed. Samia gave her refreshing take on everything, whether he wanted it or not. He'd only really had that sort of understanding with Pietro before, but now this aggravating woman had slipped into his life with her hobnail boots, her flashing eyes, and her complete and utter lack of reverence.

It didn't hurt that she managed to look stunning

in a simple blue dress, or that he found her banter appealing. She appeared to be comfortable in any situation, and with anyone, which could only make her an asset to the throne. He was pleased with his choice of bride; his only task now was to convince Samia that he would make her an ideal husband. As a seasoned seaman, he predicted stormy waters up ahead, but as he hadn't enjoyed himself or relaxed as much in a long time, so what?

Heading for his study to examine the contents of the Red Box, he was looking forward to reading about Samia. He needed flesh on the bones of what his team had told him. The two of them didn't have to be close to marry, but it was a bonus to discover a connection real and strong. Even with that, she'd have to realise that Samia would be the one making changes, not him.

CHAPTER SEVEN

WHAT TO CHOOSE...? What to choose?

She felt like a greyhound in the traps as she hovered in her dressing room, wondering what to wear. There were far too many contenders—most of which would make her feel ridiculous—for a formal dinner with Luca. Gowns with barely any fabric, held up on a wing and a prayer, were instantly discarded. The prospect of sitting next to him in one of those held zero appeal. She'd feel a right fool.

In a ferment of indecision, she thought about the hard-working crew. She didn't want to let anyone down by appearing not to care as they did. If they'd gone to the trouble to prepare a special meal, then the least she could do was to get the dress right. Obviously, Luca would look amazing, whatever he chose to wear. He could come wrapped in a towel and still look like a prince.

Actually, that wasn't such a bad idea...

Can the erotic fantasies! There isn't time, she told herself firmly.

Selecting an emerald-green gown, she slipped

it from the padded hanger. It was quite bright, and revealing by her standards, but if she was going to do this, she was going to do it properly. She didn't want Luca thinking her a shrinking violet. What use would she be then? If she was going to work her passage, he had to take her seriously.

Stroking the cobweb-fine fabric, she shook her head with sheer bemusement that anyone could afford such intricately worked clothes. The beading alone was extraordinary...so many tiny crystals, and they must all have been sewn on by hand. She had never wanted to spend her ex's money, preferring to remain independent...until he fired her from her job with the promise that she'd never work again.

We'll see about that, she mused, firming her jaw. In clothes, as in life, she had always stayed beneath the radar, except in her column where she'd spoken her mind until her ex had replaced her views with his. He still hadn't destroyed her, as he'd hoped. She was done with apologising. Luca had given her an opportunity to see a new world that she could never have dreamed of, and if she wasted that chance, she'd only have herself to blame.

Finally dressed, she turned this way and that to check her reflection. It would be hard to look bad in such a beautifully constructed gown, and she had to admit to feeling surprised by what the mirror revealed. Now it just remained for Luca to pass judgement. He'd be shocked, she imagined, as this was somewhat different from her scruffy travel clothes and beloved ancient walking boots.

Closing the door behind her, she lifted her chin and strode out.

What a dress! What a night! What a man!

What a once-in-a-lifetime opportunity!

Stepping out of an ice-cold shower that had done little to dull his raging libido, he dried off, cleaned his teeth, parked a shave, and dressed in jeans and the first top he found in the drawer. He was itching to get his hands on the contents of the Red Box, but with a lifetime of Red Boxes ahead of him—and this one wasn't going anywhere—there was a task he had to complete first. He'd come back to dress for dinner after that.

Leaving his suite, he headed for the bridge to issue new instructions. His break from hands-on sailing would last a little longer than he'd intended, though the *Black Diamond* wouldn't be heading straight back to Madlena. First, they would make a stop at a small coastal town in Italy called Portofino, where he could speak to his lawyers to make sure everything was watertight for the prenup Samia would have to sign, as well as one more document she had made necessary. He was a planner who liked to make sure every loose end was tied up. The fiesta in Portofino was wild and fabulous, and he was confident Samia would relax enough once they were there to do as he asked, and for them to get to know each other better. This was essential before he took her to Madlena to meet his people.

Having given his staff new coordinates, he left the

bridge and went to his study where the Red Box sat squat and square on his desk. Crossing the room, he extracted the key from his pocket, turned it in the lock, and tucked his finger under the lid. Swiftly riffling through the documents, he pulled out Samia's file. Opening it, he cursed his phone as it rang. Checking the caller, he took the call. A palace official wished to confirm some details concerning Luca's upcoming wedding—to the bride he had yet to propose to.

Accustomed to Luca's brother's much stiffer manner, the courtier asked tentatively, 'You do have a bride, Your Serene Highness? Only you haven't given us a name yet.'

'Discretion is always the best option,' he answered smoothly. 'I don't want the woman in question hounded by the press. But rest assured my bride does exist.'

Having exchanged the usual pleasantries, he cut the line, then stared at Samia's file, which he had put down on the desk. He'd read it later. It was better to get to know her without bias. Tonight at dinner was the perfect opportunity to do that. In a few short hours, they would moor up in Portofino, where she'd have a chance to relax and reflect on their evening together, by which time he could add whatever she had to tell him to what he'd learn about her in the file. He didn't anticipate any surprises.

It was only later in his dressing room as he adjusted his bow tie that he changed his mind. Cursing at the fiddly strip of cloth as he messed it up yet again, he let it hang loose before finally ripping it off. Reverting to jeans and a shirt, open at the neck with the cuffs rolled back, he raked his hair, which was his one concession to formal grooming. Checking his watch, he saw there was time to read Samia's file after all. Maybe he would.

She felt great, even confident in the exquisite dress as she walked across the deck towards Luca. That was weird in itself, as she'd never worn such a provocative outfit in her life. Flimsy, transparent emerald-green silk chiffon, every inch beaded with tiny shimmering crystals and lined with a nude underskirt to give the illusion that she was naked underneath, was hardly her everyday wear.

She heated beneath his glance. Then he glanced at her again and this time his stare lasted longer. Her gown was split to the waist back and front, with only proper corseting holding it together. Her cheeks were burning red under his scrutiny, but she was determined not to falter. 'Good evening,' she said evenly, relieved she didn't have high-heeled shoes to contend with as well as the figure-hugging dress.

'A very good evening,' Luca agreed, though in a disappointingly cold tone, she thought. How could he be less than enthusiastic about a night like this?

Unless something had happened since she'd last seen him.

'I feel as if I've walked through a cloud of fairy dust,' she said, smiling as she glanced around at their opulent surroundings. The dining table laid out on deck sparkled with crystal and silver, and glowed invitingly beneath the light of flickering candles. If Luca was in a grim mood, it was up to her to bring him around. Being positive and upbeat was the best way to do that. 'What a beautiful evening,' she enthused. 'A velvet sky peppered with stars, and here I am on board a fabulous black yacht slicing through the ocean.'

'Like a steel knife through butter?' he growled.

'Exactly.' She refused to be put off. 'The creak of the sails and the snap of the ropes is the only music anyone would need to make tonight perfect.'

'You think?'

Swallowing deep, she asked, 'May I sit down?'

He made a careless gesture. 'As you please.'

But he did stand politely and hold her chair to see her settled before he sat down again. Then she realised they were alone. Where was the rest of the crew? Were they to serve themselves? That would be nice...

They sat in silence for a while, which gave her the chance to mull over another puzzle. Having told her to dress for dinner, Luca was wearing banged-up jeans with his feet thrust into a pair of simple sandals. But this was the Pirate Prince, she reminded herself, and with forearms like steel girders and his wild hair tossed this way and that, what did she have to complain about? But why didn't he say something? Was she supposed to make all the chat? At least he wasn't pacing the deck. And for once, she wasn't late. *Look on the bright side*, she chided herself. *Stop looking for trouble.* But she had hoped for more.

She picked distractedly at a freshly baked roll. It was hard to maintain her optimism in the face of such obvious disapproval. Why didn't he just tell her he'd changed his mind—didn't want to have dinner with her, didn't want to talk, eat, or even be remotely civil? It was such a comedown after the laugh she'd had in her stateroom, strutting around in the fancy gown, playing the role of supersiren. The only good thing now was the banquet of delicious food laid out on the table that she couldn't face. *Let's hope he lightens up soon*, she reflected, lifting her chin, as determined as ever to make this, her first evening on board the *Black Diamond*, a good one.

Did she have to look quite so beautiful? It was like salt in a wound. He didn't trust himself to react yet. What he'd discovered in her file kept on playing through his mind on a loop.

She was what?

Who?

With a vicious curse, he'd flung the file down on the desk. He'd brought Samia on board with the best of intentions—to make her his bride, a princess, and to lavish her with gifts and a lifestyle she could only dream about. She'd been welcomed with nothing but warmth and friendship, by him and by his crew, and had made the best of impressions within minutes of being on board. Now he felt he'd betrayed his crew, his people and himself, for falling for the oldest trick in the world, which was to be made to believe that everything was exactly as it seemed. Turned out nothing was as it seemed where Samia was concerned. Her wide-eyed, apparently guileless enthusiasm was just an act.

Her file had detailed every significant event in the life of Samia Smith, newly divorced investigative journalist. No wonder his team hadn't sent that news by text. Even worse, she'd been cruelly treated by her ex-husband, her column used by that sorry excuse for a man for his own ends, but what Luca had to ask was, did a leopard ever change its spots?

An investigative journalist?

After his brother's death, he'd tried not to feel anything. There was only space in his heart for grief and guilt. Then Samia had come along, loosening him up, and bringing him back with her zany humour. That humour had lost its appeal now he knew why she'd acted as she had. Having wheedled herself onto his yacht, she had lied by omission. He got that she needed to escape a vindictive ex. He would have helped her, anyway, if she'd explained the situation. But why hadn't she told him she was a journalist? There could only be one reason, and that was to profit from it. She'd seized the main chance like everyone else. Maybe she was not a career courtesan, but she was certainly an opportunist who believed she could take him for a ride. If she imagined she was going to get away with it, she was wrong.

'Luca…?'

The conflict inside him only increased when he

drew back to stare into Samia's beautiful, lying face. How dare she look so appealing with that embarrassed expression on her face and a half shrug in her shoulders as she waited for his approval? It was dangerous to like someone as much as he liked Samia. Loving his brother, only to have him ripped away so cruelly, was the only proof he needed of that. It was better to feel nothing. Then there was nothing to lose.

'I look a mess, don't I?' she exclaimed, mouth pressing down in an apologetic smile. To make her point, she ran her hands over the figure-hugging fabric of her gown. 'Go on—you can say it,' she prompted. 'I can take it.' She pulled a comic face. 'This isn't exactly my style, is it?'

Samia thought his only problem with her was her appearance? She looked ravishing. Beyond beautiful, she was either the best actress he'd ever met, or she was seriously damaged, and he feared that the latter was the case, which meant he must protect her. The second part of the report had detailed her abuse at the hands of her husband, which angered him far more than Samia covering up her occupation ever could. But she had deceived him, and he could never forget that, though it was hard to reconcile this ingénue in her party dress with someone who would lie and cheat her way into his affection in order to get a scoop.

Don't the facts speak for themselves? Why else would she seek me out at the bar?

'I disagree,' he said curtly. 'You look beautiful.'

'Do I?' She blushed. 'Don't lie to me.'

Who was lying to whom? He prided himself on his straightforwardness. No matter what she'd done, he would not indulge in a cheap game of tit for tat.

'The gown is beautiful, as are you,' he insisted, though his tone was still clipped.

'The gown is outrageous,' she argued, laughing as her shoulders relaxed at his words. 'I'll probably fall over the fishtail train the moment I stand up.'

'I won't allow that to happen.'

'And as for getting out of it again…?' She grimaced, while he, sensibly, kept his thoughts on stripping off the gown to himself.

'Please…eat,' he insisted. 'We can talk later.'

They would talk later.

At length.

Her blush deepened as stewards came silently from the shadows to attend them at the dinner table. How much had they heard? As bad as it was to suffer Luca's obvious displeasure, it was worse to think they'd been overheard. That was the price royalty, and those close to royals, must endure, she reasoned. Everything came with a price, and a complete lack of privacy was perhaps the highest price of all to pay.

'The champagne is open.' Luca indicated the misted bottle as a steward removed the cork with barely the faintest pop. 'Would you like a glass?'

'I don't think I should,' she admitted on a short laugh. 'I'm having enough trouble walking in this tight-fitting gown without adding alcohol to the mix.'

'One glass won't hurt,' he said curtly.

And might loosen her tongue enough for her to tell him the truth—that she'd had enough of his moody behaviour, and if he didn't want her here, he just had to say so.

'Thank you. I'll call you if I need anything else,' Luca told the stewards. 'We'll serve ourselves this evening.'

It was hard not to brood on Luca's mood, so to distract them both she produced the report he'd asked for.

'What report is this?' he demanded impatiently.

'The yacht's décor,' she reminded him. 'I'm no expert, but I do have an opinion. I wrote my ideas down longhand. I hope that's all right? My handwriting's not the best, but you should be able to read it…'

'You really have no idea, do you?' he asked.

'About interior décor? No. Honestly, I don't, but I have an opinion, as I said, and I thought that's what you wanted to hear. Anyway, here it is,' she said, pushing it across the table to him.

He brushed it aside. 'I've no time for this. I have something more pressing on my mind.'

'Can I help you with that?'

'Oh, yes, I think you can.'

'I realise you'd rather be sailing,' she agreed, 'than sitting here with—'

'An investigative journalist?' he bit out.

CHAPTER EIGHT

As Samia's jaw dropped on hearing his accusation, he wondered if the cause was innocent shock, or guilt? Either way, she had deceived him, and was continuing to do so. He had to sort this out before anything else could happen. 'Did you seriously imagine I wouldn't find out?'

She tensed as she closed her eyes, and then she released a long, steadying breath. 'It's not what you think.'

'Really?' he challenged, unmoved. 'And what do I think? Or, should I say, what would you like me to think?'

'That isn't fair,' she insisted hotly. 'We met by chance.'

'And I'm supposed to believe that?'

'You gave me the opportunity to get away.'

'Nice story, Samia, but it would have been more honest for you to tell me the truth from the start. Would you care to hear my version of events?'

'I'd like that very much,' she said, lifting her chin.

'Coming across me by accident in that particular bar seems unlikely. I think you were tipped off.'

'By whom?'

'Does it matter?'

'I didn't know anyone in the bar until I met you.'

'So you say.'

'Because it's true.' Firming her jaw, she fired back, 'Next question?'

'You wheedled your way onto my yacht with your story about wanting a job.'

'First off, I didn't *wheedle*,' she told him with a steely look. 'You invited me onto your yacht. And I don't *want* a job. I *need* a job,' she corrected him firmly. 'Which is something you seem reluctant to give me, though I noticed no reluctance on your part when you first invited me to join you on board.'

Not expecting this level of defiance from someone who was so clearly guilty, he leaned in. 'So you won't benefit from your voyage on board the *Black Diamond*? Is that what you want me to believe?'

'Believe what you like. I can't change your mind, but I'd like to know why you're so mistrustful.' Angling her chin, she waited for him to reply, as if he was being grilled now.

'Nice try,' he rapped crisply, 'but don't try and turn this on me.'

Rising, she planted her tiny fists on the table, and, lowering her head, she stared him straight in the eyes. 'I know your brother died, leaving you to pick up the pieces, but I'm not responsible for that tragedy.'

She might as well have slapped him across the face. He recoiled as if she had. No one dared to mention his brother's death to his face. No one intruded on his grief.

'I don't know who's responsible for the tragedy,' she continued grimly, apparently unaware of his mounting fury. 'Since we've met, I've looked back over the old reports about his death on the Internet. There was an embargo on the facts in the press, as I'm sure you know. I strongly suspect you lost your brother the same way I lost my mother, although I don't expect you to admit it. But whatever you've been through—and I know you've been through a lot—you're not the only one. I also know what it's like to lose a loved one—'

She broke off and her mouth worked. She said nothing for quite a while. Samia would be remembering her mother's death, and fighting down her feelings. He remained silent in respect for her grief, even as anger for her deception continued to seethe inside him.

'Whatever you went through doesn't give you the right to hold me to account for your feelings now,' she maintained.

Standing, he slammed his own fists down on the table. 'Enough! We end this now.'

'That would be too easy,' she countered fiercely. Craning her chin, she glared into his eyes. 'How about we both come clean?' she challenged.

Passion couldn't have been higher. The atmosphere they had created between them was thick with

unresolved anger. Even the sea breeze that had stiffened into a gusting wind and lashed them remorse-
lessly didn't stand a chance of cooling things down.

'You're hiding something too,' she insisted tightly.

'And you want to write the story,' he derided. One
emotion crowned the other, until it was like a lava
plug ready to blow.

'How shockingly mistrustful you are,' she accused angrily.

'Do you blame me?'

The tragedy of his brother's death had been shocking enough, but to discover Pietro had taken his own
life, and that Luca had not been there to talk him
down and help him, was a wound he would endure
for the rest of his life. It had ripped the emotional
rug from under his feet, leaving him shipwrecked
with nothing to cling to but raw passion. And he was
done with slamming fists down on a table. Samia
had known enough violence in her life. She might
rile him like no one else, but whatever else he was,
or was not, he was no bully. What he'd learned about
Samia and her ex wasn't bland, it wasn't regular, and
it had forced him to balance his relief that she had
escaped an abusive relationship intact with the very
real threat that an investigative journalist presented
to the throne. No royal house could afford to take
a cuckoo into its nest, especially when that cuckoo
had direct links to the media.

'What else did you hope to gain, apart from your
story?' he demanded.

'What are you getting at?' she bit back.

The wind whipped them mercilessly as they stood glaring at each other. 'Money from your story?' he suggested. 'Or perhaps it was even simpler than that.'

'Meaning?'

'Your ex was rich, but I am richer.'

Shaking her head, she made an incredulous sound. 'That isn't worthy of you, Luca. I'll freely admit my ex-husband wasn't in your league, but who is? There's extreme wealth and then there's…' She glanced around at all the accoutrements that went into making a billion-euro yacht. 'Plus, you have the weight of history on your side,' she added as she speared him with a furious look. 'As well as a duty to care for your people.'

'Which I fully intend to do,' he gritted out.

'And you think they need protection from me? Or are you more interested in protecting yourself from a predatory woman?'

'Are you a predatory woman?'

'I'm whatever I need to be,' she admitted with the steel he was becoming used to. 'But would I knowingly profit from others? No. I stand on my own two feet, and have done for years. I made a major mistake when I married my ex, thinking I could save my parents. But I never make the same mistake twice, so you can rest assured that if bread and butter is all I can afford, then bread and butter is all I eat.'

'So you're not after my money.'

'Didn't I just say that?'

'And you disapprove of all this…' It was his turn to gesture around.

'It's a completely different world for me,' she admitted, 'but do I disapprove? No. Why should I? You don't expect other people to pay for your pleasure. You've earned it.'

Silence stretched between them. At first it was hostile and tense, but then gradually they both came down from the peak of fury to a sort of understanding.

'I could only dream of sailing a boat like this when I was a boy,' he admitted. 'Madlena was impoverished when my parents came to the throne. They built it into the country it is, but at the start I had no expectation of being entitled to anything beyond what I could earn for myself. If you know anything about me, you should remember that my tech company was a start-up in my bedroom—'

'On a second-hand computer, which you restored,' she supplied.

'So you read up about me as well as Pietro.'

'You don't hold the monopoly on researching those you meet, and I applaud you for refinancing your country to the benefit of your people before you thought of doing anything for yourself,' she said coolly.

'I'm not so bad, after all?'

'Maybe that applies to both of us?' she suggested.

'When were you going to tell me what you did?' he countered. 'What you still do, or hope to continue doing, is my best guess. Or did you intend to hide the fact that you used to write for a national newspaper in the UK, and had an extremely popular and highly respected column?'

'*Used to* being the operative phrase,' she admitted with a rueful huff. 'My ex kicked me out when he had no further use for me, saying I had ten minutes to clear my desk. I was marched out of the building by his security staff like a common thief.'

'When were you going to tell me?' he repeated.

'When the time was right.'

'Pillow talk?'

'Does that sound like me?'

'I don't know too much about you,' he pointed out.

'Or I about you,' she conceded.

'Are you here to spy on me, Samia Smith?'

'No. I am not,' she stated firmly. 'I'll admit I was curious about you, and excited to learn how the super-rich live, but isn't everyone curious about that, and for purely innocent reasons? I didn't set out with the intention to share what I learned with the rest of the world.'

'How can I be sure?'

'You can't,' she said frankly.

'So, you're asking me to believe you came here out of idle curiosity?'

'And to escape,' she reminded him forthrightly. 'My ex was a bully, a very nasty, vindictive man. You don't have to believe me, but that's the truth.'

'And now I must consider the possibility that you have realised the many opportunities that have opened up since you met me, both to re-establish yourself and to further your career. You'd be a fool not to seize that chance.'

'Yet like you, I have principles,' she countered, 'so I guess we both have to learn to trust.'

'You're asking me to trust you not to write about me?'

'As I have to trust you not to hurt me.'

That shocked him more than anything else she might have said. He would never hurt her, but he had to put his country and its people first, which meant he must be sure that his choice of bride was as good as he'd first thought it. 'We'll have to come to an accommodation.'

'Meaning what?' she demanded suspiciously. 'I won't sleep with you to seal the deal, if that's what you think.' And when his brow shot up, she added, 'Sex means a lot more to me than that.'

'Fear and loathing?' She blushed as he said it. 'I've read your file.'

'You had my personal life investigated?'

'Of course,' he admitted. 'This is not just about my personal safety, but the well-being of a country and its people. Our original deal was for you to come on board the *Black Diamond* in search of a job. At no point do I remember inviting you to interview for the post of mistress.' As she visibly swallowed, he knew Samia must be wondering if she had left one bad situation only to walk straight into another. 'It's never been my intention to intimidate you, or force you to remain here with me. My plan has always been to fashion a deal we're both happy to subscribe to.'

'I don't understand what this *deal* is. What do you expect of me? You haven't specified a job yet.'

'For now I ask only one thing, and that is not to tar me with the same brush as your ex.'

About whom he knew everything.

'My lawyers will ensure that—' *that the self-important, pasty-faced barrel of lard my people have described to me would never beat up a woman again* '—he will never hurt you again.' His guts twisted at the thought of Samia trapped in a loveless marriage with such a brute.

'What have you done?'

She looked genuinely frightened, which for Samia was a rare loss of composure. The fiend she'd married had clearly done some serious damage to a woman who deserved so much more.

'Don't look so worried. I'm not a thug and I don't employ criminals so let's just say I have contacts in all the right places, and can promise you that, from this moment on, you will be safe from him.'

She let this sink in for a moment and then asked the obvious question. 'And what do you expect from me in exchange for your protection?'

He let the waters settle before explaining. 'This is not about protection. The word alone makes it sound as if you're a bird trapped in a cage, dependent on me for everything that keeps you alive, when I know you're a tiger that can care for itself perfectly well.'

It took Samia a few moments to realise he was

serious, and then she thanked him with a perplexed frown. 'And you?' she said at last. 'How will you deal with having an investigative journalist alongside you on this voyage?'

Their association would last a lot longer than that, if he had his way. But she did have a point. For a stranger, let alone a journalist, to get this close to the Pirate Prince had been thought impossible, and anything Samia could find out would be beyond value to the press. She only had to use him as a headline for her credibility to be restored. She could name her price, choose any newspaper she liked, and have its top people begging her to put her by-line on a column.

'I think you're ambitious,' he agreed thoughtfully, 'but not to snare a wealthy husband, or you'd have stayed where you were, and not just for a one-week wonder in the press. I think you're looking for a lot more than that.'

'Of course I am,' she agreed hotly.

'Self-fulfilment and independence,' he mused out loud.

'If you mean I don't look to anyone to support me or to validate me, and that I take pride in working and achieving, and loving and caring, you're right, but to do that I have to be free to be my own person, free of all influence.'

'And intimidation,' he added significantly.

Clouds invaded her eyes, as she no doubt thought back. 'Of course,' she whispered, but she quickly rallied. 'I can't live in a cage, however lush, and I won't *ever* live in fear again.'

There was quite a pause before he felt it was right to intrude on her memories, but then he asked the question uppermost in his mind. 'Could you be a princess?'

Samia gazed at him askance. 'I'm *sorry*?'

'What better way to restore your credibility than with your first-hand story of life with the Pirate Prince?'

'As your wife?' She gasped, incredulous as his meaning sank in. 'You really imagine I'd write about you, if I were your wife?'

An ironic smile crept onto his lips. 'Exactly.'

'And we were just starting to get back on an even keel. Why did you have to spoil it?' she demanded with a tense laugh. 'Except, of course, I know you're teasing.'

'Who said I'm teasing?'

'You are. You have to be. Unless you've gone completely crazy.'

'Portofino tomorrow,' he stated evenly. 'There's a fiesta. That should lighten things up.'

Samia's tolerant sigh said it would take a lot more than a party to persuade her that his suggestion was anything more than a joke.

CHAPTER NINE

'THE FIESTA WILL be hectic,' Luca had warned her as he stood up from the table that night. 'You'll need a good night's sleep...'

She was supposed to sleep after what he'd said? *Princess* Samia? It didn't even sound right. Turning over in bed for the umpteenth time, she punched her hapless pillow into submission. As she did so, she saw the glorious emerald-green gown, discarded where she'd stepped out of it. The beading glistened in the moonlight as if mocking her attempt to turn into an irresistible siren overnight. 'Well, that fell flat,' she muttered, flopping over so she didn't have to look at the gown. She'd had more success with a cotton dress!

A smile crept onto her mouth at the thought. Wasn't that a point in Luca's favour? He didn't even have to try. Snug-fitting jeans, and a shirt caressing his immensely powerful shoulders—why, even his feet looked sexy in a pair of cheap sandals he'd probably picked up at a market. But it was his eyes that really did the damage. They shot heat straight to her core.

It was as if he'd cast an erotic net and she had swum right into it, she mused as she snuggled lower in the bed. Every part of her body had responded with approval, whether he chose to be pleasant or not. And they had got heated last night. Though, they'd mellowed out after he'd told her she would live fear-free from now on. That was worth everything. But then he'd had to go and spoil it with that ridiculous suggestion. Princess indeed! And he'd probably be sleeping like a baby…

That was all she remembered until someone hammered on her door.

'Get up, if you want to visit Portofino,' Luca called out.

'Give me half an hour,' she called back groggily. 'I'll see you on deck.'

'Ten minutes,' he called back, 'and then we're leaving with or without you.'

The day was young and undecided, but the sound of Luca's voice was the only encouragement she needed to leap out of bed and rush to the shower. She didn't even bother to dry her hair. Having towelled it, she raked it with her fingers and heaped it on top of her head. Shoving a clip in to hold it in place, she turned to the sink, where cleaning her teeth took a lot longer than doing her hair. *Well, you never know…*

Yes, she did, Samia lectured her inner voice patiently. Luca was indulging her with this invitation to visit Portofino, but that didn't mean there were kisses in store.

Worse luck, she mused wryly as she slicked on some lip gloss. She'd been dreading all contact with men, but Luca had succeeded in filling her with a simmering hunger, as well as a desperate need to discover if things could be different—if *she* could be different—when it came to full-on sex.

Perhaps it was just as well she had no time to progress those thoughts.

Slipping on another sundress from the hoard in the box at the back of the wardrobe, she grabbed a purse that sighed mournfully, rather than chinked merrily. It couldn't be helped. At least she didn't have to pay for the lift to and from shore.

Shoving her feet into a pair of flip-flops she'd found alongside the box of sundresses, she headed out, by which time she was bubbling with excitement at the thought of spending the day with Luca, and exploring a new place together.

Luca was cool. His crew was around, she reasoned, and he hadn't exactly fussed over her last night. Which was how she liked it, she told herself firmly. What he'd said about keeping her safe was far more important. And it meant she didn't have to face her greatest fear. It was one thing fantasising about Luca introducing her to a better kind of sex, and another thing actually doing it. Anyway, he didn't seem interested in exacting that sort of payment for the voyage, which was a relief.

Was it?

The Pirate Prince looked hotter than ever this morning in a pair of black surf shorts and a form-fitting, sleeveless top that showed off his muscles to perfection. One day, maybe she'd find the courage to forget the humiliation of failure as far as the bedroom went, and find something fulfilling in the experience with someone she really cared about... someone who understood her fears. She could only dream that might be Luca. But reality was never that kind.

As before, he took charge of making sure she was safely transferred over the churning sea from the *Black Diamond* to the rolling powerboat. He steadied her with his hand on her forearm while she made the transition, and his touch was like an incendiary device to her senses. It made her pulse race and her breathing quicken—which he noticed, of course.

'Are you scared or excited?' he asked as she staggered to the prow on the bucking boat under his guidance.

'I'm neither scared nor excited. Well, maybe a little excited,' she conceded.

'Only a little?'

Her body heated instantly at the sight of a glimmer of a smile on his mouth. Luca only had to look at her like that for years of doubt and dread to melt away, to be replaced by a throbbing yearning. Her dress was thin, and her body was a notoriously unreliable keeper of secrets, so, however much she tried to brazen it out, the brush of his arm against hers caused her nipples to tighten, while her lips felt swollen and tender beneath the tip of her tongue.

Clearing her throat, she told him briskly, 'You must tell me if I can be of any help on shore.'

'Fetching and carrying? Or did you have something else in mind?'

'I don't care so long as I'm earning my passage.'

'Keep me entertained,' he said in a disappointingly disinterested tone. 'That's your only job today.'

'Court jester?' she suggested.

To her relief, Luca's dark gaze flared briefly with something that might have been humour. 'If the cap fits.'

'I'll only wear it if it's got bells on it.'

'That can be arranged.' His lips twitched. He almost cracked a smile.

By the time they disembarked in Portofino, he'd decided to stay an extra day. He'd been on the move long enough, and so had Samia. The small town had lost none of its picturesque charm in all the years he'd been coming here, and he wanted to show her around. For someone who'd been trapped in London in a loveless marriage, the starburst of exuberance that unfolded in front of them could only be the best possible tonic. If he wanted a bride and he wanted that bride to be Samia, uninterested as he had always been in prolonging any relationship, or even working on it, this was worth it... She was worth it. Better used to *arrangements* swiftly made between him and an experienced woman—with no need for preliminaries, because they both chose to cut straight to the chase—he knew that would never be enough to convince Samia to marry him. In fact, it would probably have the opposite effect. She'd need more than a nice meal and sex. A lot more, he reflected, taking in her shining eyes as she viewed the scene.

The tiny harbour town of Portofino was bathed in sunshine when they arrived. The sky was unrelieved blue, while the fresh sea air was filled with the scent of blossoms cascading exuberantly over wrought-iron balconies. As they approached the main area lined with cafés, she was greeted by the signature scent of the region, which was lemon in all its various guises. Every table they passed seemed to be decorated with lemons and lemon leaves, both as a symbol of the region and to entice the customer to sit down and linger a while.

'Drink?' Luca invited.

'Yes, please.'

He ordered the ingredients for a local speciality, which was lemon juice, sugar, or sweetener, and fresh spring water, which the customers were left to mix themselves to taste. A jug of ice was delivered to the table, and half the fun was agreeing how much of each ingredient they should add. It was hard to be tense while she and Luca were arguing over the best recipe.

'Taste,' he instructed, holding the glass to her lips.

'Delicious!' He was definitely more pirate than prince today—and the drink was tasty too. 'But mine is better,' she insisted.

Leaning over, Luca took a sip. 'Not bad,' he conceded.

'Mine's better,' she threw back with a smile.

He leaned forward, his dark eyes smouldering into hers, and for the briefest moment she wondered if he was going to kiss her, but then he stood and went to pay the bill. Luca was playing her as a virtuoso might play a violin, she thought as she admired his back view. The Pirate Prince was impossibly attractive. As well as tricky to deal with, she concluded as she stood up, and he politely moved her chair away so they could continue their tour of Portofino.

She decided within the first hour that the fiesta was a full-on ravishment of the senses. The town was very pretty with its big wide square, cobbled streets leading off, and a walkway around the bay, lined with tiny boutiques, bars and restaurants. Festooned with bunting and banners, and with several bands competing for an audience, it was the noisiest and most wonderful celebration. Crowded with people of all ages, dressed in their best beneath mellow sunshine, and with stallholders calling out their wares, everyone was smiling. The scent of fresh bread, still warm from the oven, made her mouth water as they passed a stall, while other stalls boasted cheeses and cakes, as well as ice cream that made her sigh with anticipation. Having Luca at her side was like the icing on the thick slice of panettone, the sweet buttery fruit-filled bread he insisted she must try.

The crowds thickened as they walked on, and

then he stopped outside a lawyers' office. 'These people act for me,' he explained.

'Would you like me to wait outside?'

'No. You come in,' he said.

Nice of him not to keep her waiting on the street, she thought as he opened the door of a very traditional-looking office, full of mahogany panelling, tiled floors, and the evocative scent of beeswax. 'Do you have an appointment?'

'They're expecting me. And you as well.'

'Me?' she exclaimed with surprise.

'I'd like you to sign something.'

Of course.

She met his gaze and held it levelly. 'A non-disclosure agreement?' she guessed.

'Do you have any objections?'

'None.' But she wished he'd trusted her enough to discuss it with her first. But then again, why should he? She'd kept the truth about being an investigative journalist from Luca, until he'd uncovered the information for himself, so she could hardly refuse his request now.

The wood-panelled room they were shown into boasted no distracting views of the sea. Instead, it was a small space for a keen mind to work in. The lawyer explained exactly what she was about to sign, and insisted on taking her through the agreement line by line.

She was actually very happy to sign it, thinking it might release a lot of tension that had built up between her and Luca.

'I'm sorry I had to ask you to do that,' he said stiffly as they stepped back into the lemon-scented air.

'It's fine. I totally understand your reasons.'

'Well, thank you for being so understanding.'

It was tense for a while after that, and she felt it was up to her to lighten the mood. 'Let's move on,' she suggested, meaning more than just walking down the street.

'Agreed,' Luca said.

For the rest of the day he was the perfect companion, and proved to be as competitive as she was, when it came to the shooting gallery and some of the other stalls. They tried all the games, even the coconut shy, where she proved to have quite an accurate aim, which meant they left the pitch laughing with their arms full of fluffy toys. 'This must be quite a change from your high-tech empire?'

'Something to remember when I return home,' Luca agreed.

'The children of Madlena would love something like this fiesta.'

Taking that as his cue, Luca began to hand out the toys they'd won to parents walking by.

'Job well done,' she said when he returned to her side.

'How about dancing?'

She had two left feet, but why not? There were a lot of things she wanted to do with Luca Fortebracci, but luckily she had more sense. Dancing was safe.

Or she had always thought it was.

The moment she stepped into Luca's arms, everything else faded away. There was barely time for the vague impression that they were standing close on a tightly packed dance floor to register before Luca's arms were wrapped around her with no pretence at keeping things the right side of safe. She couldn't think straight. She didn't want to think at all. All that mattered was remembering how this felt, and carrying those feelings forward into the future to keep her company when she was alone again. The rhythm of the band was sultry, and the melody tugged at her heart. It made her want things she couldn't have, like Luca, and like being part of one of the happy families milling around them. Why couldn't life be like this all the time?

Because then you wouldn't appreciate moments like these, she told herself impatiently, wishing she weren't such a softie beneath her protective shell, and could let her tears fall freely. She wasn't sad. This was too much happiness. No strings, no expectation on either side, no titles, no nobodies, just Samia and Luca enjoying a dance in the village square.

She acted cool, but was secretly thrilled when Luca kept his arm looped loosely around her waist as the band segued from one tune to another. Her imagination got to work right away... Luca tightening his grip, claiming her, caring for her, loving her.

'You okay?' he asked, as she gave an unintentional, but decidedly blissful sigh.

This girl doesn't do begging, she reminded herself as Luca stared down into her face, their lips just inches apart. But she did do a lot of dreaming, and no one could stop her doing that.

Having Samia in his arms as they danced had sharpened Luca's senses to an almost painful degree. Their bodies brushed lightly as they moved to the music. He made sure that was all they would do. He could wait. The longer he waited, the hungrier they would be, and pleasure should never be rushed. When Samia came to him, he wanted her wild with need and full of trust. He wanted to meet that tiger caged inside her and feel its claws. After another hour or so of the fiesta, they'd return to the ship. His lawyers knew to expect him again the following morning, when he would be ready to make arrangements to ensure that his return to Madlena would be with a bride. Today was for relaxing, so Samia was in the right frame of mind when he made his formal proposal.

She sighed as the band stopped playing and laid down their instruments to take a break. 'I don't want this to end.'

She looked so innocent and happy, he could almost believe this was a conventional courtship. 'Would you like to return to the yacht for dinner?'

'More food?' She laughed.

'You could wear another of those fabulous gowns.'

'Or shorts?' she proposed as they began to stroll back towards the quay. 'To be honest, I feel silly in those dresses.'

'Well, you don't look silly,' he said firmly. 'You look like a princess.'

She gave an incredulous laugh. 'That'll be the day.'

He decided not to pursue the princess theme as they walked back. All that mattered was that Samia was happy and relaxed, her eyes bright with anticipation at the thought of the night ahead. He realised he was beginning to care for her. She suited his purpose when it came to his hunt for a bride, but it was something more than that that made him smile.

They didn't make it as far as their respective staterooms. Something had changed between them. For him, it was unrequited lust and extreme pain in the groin region, while for Samia it was possibly an expression of relief at signing the non-disclosure agreement, which meant they could put their differences behind them and move on, though he liked to think it might be lust on her part too.

They stood side by side but not touching on board the powerboat taking them back. They boarded his yacht without incident, but a tension he knew only too well had started building. It seemed like the most natural thing on earth to link their fingers as they began to walk through the ship. Their steady pace didn't last long, and soon he was pulling her along behind him as if their lives depended on it.

CHAPTER TEN

HER THROAT WAS dry with excitement, her breathing all over the place. This was wrong. *This was right.* She didn't know what the heck it was, but if she waited for the right moment to come along, it might never happen. And if it did, but not with Luca, would she regret missing out for the rest of her life?

Walls, doors, companionways rushed past. Everything became a blur. Then he stopped dead and, whirling her around, he pinned her to the wall with his fists planted either side of her head. She was still in midyelp of surprise when his black eyes asked one question: *Do you want this?*

Having seen all he needed to, Luca continued to lead her on down the corridor. When they reached the companionway leading to the upper deck, he went ahead, and then stopped and turned to face her. Without the slightest hesitation she moved into his arms. Lifting her, he shouldered his way into the first door they came across. Kicking it shut behind them, he secured the lock. Carrying her across a glorious, jewel-coloured Persian rug, in what was a very smart-looking office, he lowered her onto the desk. Nudging his way between her legs, he made her cry out with pleasure at his first touch, and that was just his thigh brushing against her. There was no mistaking how much he wanted her. Moving deeper, he dipped at the knees and slowly drew himself up again, so she could enjoy the full benefit of his erection. Beneath the placket of his surf shorts, she could feel every inch of his firm length and incredible breadth. The prospect of knowing him intimately drew a whimper of excitement from her throat. The wealth of hard muscle beneath her hands, together with Luca's knowing attention to that sensitive place between her legs, gave her an overload of sensation, and before she could stop herself she lost control.

'That's good,' he breathed as she bucked helplessly in his arms while pleasure rampaged through her body. She cried out in time to each exquisite spasm, until finally they subsided and she collapsed, gasping with shocked delight in Luca's arms.

There was no brushing of lips or tender exploration, and none needed. Luca drove his mouth down on hers, and she responded with matching fire. No longer two people reeling from the unexpected hand of cards that life had dealt them, a woman fearful of penetrative sex, and a man mourning the loss of his brother, they were feral creatures in the prime of life feeding greedily off each other's hunger.

'I want more,' she gasped, writhing and thrusting to prove it. Having been denied any semblance of enjoyment in the physical side of marriage, she was desperate to try everything Luca could teach her. The urge to pleasure him in return was just as strong. Slipping her hands beneath his top, she pulled up the fabric to kiss his hot skin. Tanned, salty, and hard with muscle, Luca was everything she'd expected and more, and the taste of him pushed her arousal higher. He responded by tugging down the straps of her sundress to expose her breasts, but even though she strained towards him, he denied her his touch where she wanted it, and only teased her with kisses on her neck, and on her shoulders.

'Oh, please, more,' she begged, feeling as if her nipples were screaming for attention.

Luca laughed softly, down deep in his throat, while she urged him on with guttural sounds of need. The way he used his tongue and teeth to tease her mouth, her lips, made heat flash to her core. She was as hungry as if she hadn't experienced the ultimate pleasure only minutes before. It still wasn't enough. She had to feel him skin to skin.

A cry of excitement escaped her throat when Luca ripped off his top and flung it across the room. Holding his fierce stare, she issued a challenge of her own. Pulling her dress over her head, she dared him to mock her as her ex had. *They'll bruise your knees when you're older*, he had used to sneer, referring to her generous breasts, but Luca was openly admiring.

'Magnificent...' he whispered, cupping them and weighing them appreciatively as he chafed her nipples with the lightest of touches.

Throwing her head back, she moaned, 'More...'

'Don't worry, I haven't finished with you yet,' he promised as a sigh of pure pleasure shuddered out of her.

'I need this,' she somehow managed to gasp.

'I know it,' he confirmed huskily.

He understood her need and his voice was pure seduction in itself. When he reached for the catch on her bra, she shifted position to help him. Wriggling out of it, she made his job easy, but if there was one thing she had learned about Luca, it was that he was never predictable. Her knickers were discarded next, and, dropping to his knees in front of her, he parted her legs and brought them to rest on his shoulders. With a groan of anticipation, she relaxed back onto the desk, leaning on her forearms for support. Papers went flying this way and that, and a big red box went crashing to the ground. 'Leave it,' Luca growled as he supported her buttocks to lift her to his mouth.

He was right. Nothing mattered. Nothing could, she reflected dazedly as she drifted into a world where pleasure ruled. Could she survive this? She wondered as Luca explored her with his tongue. The sensation was indescribable. How did he know how to do this, and to do it so well? She ground her body against his mouth, knowing there was no hope of holding on, and no reason to, so she didn't even try. Her world shattered into a rhythmical starburst explosion of sensation, while she cried out as each pulse of pleasure gripped her, with her fingers laced through Luca's hair.

'More?' he suggested wryly when she was finally quiet.

What do you think? banged in her brain, but she couldn't drag in enough air to say the words. The best she could do was to express herself in sensual sounds of need.

'Empty your mind and relax every muscle,' he instructed as he spread her legs wide.

'Yes,' she agreed eagerly. She would agree to anything now.

'Don't hold back,' he advised.

As if she could!

Closing her eyes and thinking of nothing but sensation intensified the experience. Taking his time, Luca teased her back to a state of full arousal where he kept her suspended until she was as hungry for pleasure as if she'd never been fed.

'So, so good,' she gasped as he upped the pace of his mind-shatteringly skilful lapping. Changing his grip on her buttocks so he could use one hand to pleasure her, he lifted her to a new level with delicate feather-light strokes of his finger pad. That, added to the exquisite pressure of his tongue, tipped her over the edge again, and she fell, shrieking with relief as each powerful pleasure wave gripped her.

She was still hazy minded with the afterglow when he gathered her into his arms. He didn't say anything, he didn't need to, he just held her and stroked her, and kissed her as he soothed her down.

'We will talk later,' he promised in a tone she'd

never heard him use before. 'But take your time,' he added gently, 'I won't rush you.'

'Into what?' she asked with a frown.

Pulling back, she stared deep into Luca's eyes. She was calm, and she was drowsy and contented, but when someone went out of his way to be considerate, her past history made her suspicious. Her ex had been a perfect example. When he wanted something, he could be particularly nice. What did Luca want?

'I won't rush you into dinner,' he explained with one of his dangerous smiles.

'Okay.' But something still niggled at the back of her mind.

Scooping up her clothes, Luca held them while she dressed. She couldn't fault him for politeness. Her only concern was that everything seemed to be happening in such a rush. Getting to this stage in a relationship took weeks usually, but with Luca her control was out of the window.

'I'll see you at dinner,' he said as he turned for the door, 'and we'll talk.'

The offer was both a promise and a puzzle. What did he want to talk about? Her job on board? He seemed in no hurry to assign her any duties.

A leisurely bath and a good think were called for, she decided, to work out where she was going from here. Luca's expression gave her nothing to worry about. It was warm, sexy, brooding...and settled, as if she had inadvertently answered a question. Had he thought she was frigid too? And was that the only thing on his mind? She wasn't frigid, but she was frightened of penetrative sex, and with good reason. Her ex had been a brute and a bully with no thought for anyone but himself.

'Shall I escort you back to your cabin?' Luca suggested, resting his hand lightly on her shoulder.

His comment shook her out of these thoughts and returned a smile to her face. 'I can still walk—just.'

'Don't get lost,' he cautioned, matching the warmth of her smile.

Too late. She was already lost. Now they'd started down this road, she wasn't interested in detours.

Her mood had changed by the time she reached her suite. A feeling of uncertainty was growing. She wanted Luca with a fierce longing, while common sense told her it could never be. His joke about her being a princess was just that—his idea of humour. Why he even wanted to keep her around was a bit of a mystery. It wasn't as if he'd got anything out of their sexual encounter. For her it was an exercise in trust. Giving herself…showing her most vulnerable self to Luca in that moment of release was huge. Trust in another human being didn't come bigger than that. Her ex had planted so many seeds of self-doubt inside her, but if she were that frigid, overweight pain in the ass he'd always called her, why did Luca want to be with her? There could be no faking that run through the ship, when hunger for each other had gripped them equally. And why would he trouble to give her so much pleasure and demand nothing for himself? She'd seen no mockery in his eyes, heard no scathing note in his voice. There hadn't been a single unkind comment. Quite the opposite, in fact.

Throughout everything, she remained a hopeless romantic, she decided, while Luca was a pragmatist with a disciplined, logical mind. Was she just another of the Pirate Prince's casual love affairs, and, if that were the case, was she happy to stick around until he tired of her? That didn't strike her as being captain of her ship and taking her destiny into her own hands.

Maybe she should cut them both some slack, Samia concluded. There was huge change looming in Luca's life. Of course he was living every day to the full. He had advised her to do the same, so why didn't she?

Sex was an exercise at which Luca excelled, and that was all it had ever been to him in the past. Samia had changed that, changed him. He had never been so determined to pleasure a woman, or felt so consumed by desire that common sense had deserted him. The deal between them was supposed to be straightforward, an agreement that brought benefits to both parties. He gained a bride to reassure his people that his days of rampaging were over, while Samia was free to do as she pleased. Free from fear of her ex-husband, who was already being dealt with by Luca's lawyers, and free from money worries for the rest of her life. She would join him in Madlena as a princess of that country for as long as it suited them both.

All well and good so far, but what he hadn't factored into his plan was caring for her to this extent. And now it was too late. Samia in the throes of passion had changed her, but it had also changed him. Her vulnerability in those moments had touched him. After all she'd been through, she had chosen to show her raw self to him. He'd always been able to switch off his feelings before. Why couldn't he do that now? As a child, he had quickly come to understand that he could never be as precious as his brother, the heir. Pietro had helped him to accept this, and when their parents were killed, and first his grandmother, and then Pietro had assumed responsibility for Luca's welfare, Luca's main aim had been not to put any additional burden on his brother. That was why he'd chosen a career in special forces, while Pietro had taken the role that would eventually suck the lifeblood out of him.

He'd been out of the country on yet another covert mission when Pietro took his own life. His brother's note had explained that the pressure of ruling a country was too much for him, and that Luca would make a far better Prince than he had. Luca lived with that guilt, and it made his concern for Samia all the more intense. He'd been on the point of proposing when she broke apart in his arms, but, remembering how impatient he'd often been with his brother when Pietro had doubted himself, he couldn't rush something so important now. Samia was so much more than he'd thought her, but instead of intimacy clearing his head, as it usually did, she had only doubled his distractions. Outwardly vulnerable, even prim, she had a very different side to her character, and he was more determined than ever to set that part of her free.

The discovery of a simple column of ivory silk tucked away between all the glitz and glamour hanging in her dressing room thrilled Samia. Sleeveless and ankle-length, with a boat neck that exposed her shoulders rather than her breasts, it had a split up one side, but only to just above the knee. The fabric felt lovely, and as light as air as she slipped it on over a lacy bra and thong.

She found Luca at the bow rail, dressed in jeans and a top. His hair was still damp from his shower, and the stubble that had abraded her mouth when he'd kissed her was thicker than ever. Swinging around at her approach, he exclaimed, 'Excuse my appearance. I've been up the mast making repairs, and I lost track of time.'

And must have ripped off his clothes and dived under the shower, she mused, picturing the scene as she took in his glorious body.

'You look amazing,' he commented matter-of-factly.

'You like the dress?'

'It's a great improvement on the sparkling cucumber you wore last time.'

She laughed and relaxed. 'That green dress must have cost a fortune.'

'Then someone clearly wasted their money—and I'm sorry to say that was me. While *this* vision of loveliness...' walking up close, he took hold of her hands and held out her arms to admire her chosen outfit '...is worth every penny.'

The touch of his lips on hers, his hands on her body, his clean man scent, and warm minty breath and the fire in his dangerous black eyes were everything she could ever want. When Luca kissed her, she felt complete. He stirred her emotions and filled her with fire.

'I thought we'd eat here on deck,' Luca said, indicating the comfortable casual seating area. 'We can serve ourselves beneath the stars.'

'Perfect.' What could be better, especially when they were both so relaxed?

But he got down to business right away. 'I hope you haven't had second thoughts about signing that document?' he said as they sat down.

Yes, it niggled. She'd be lying if she denied it. She didn't like being thought of as untrustworthy, but she could see that Luca had to protect himself and his country. 'I can't say I like the necessity of it,' she admitted, 'but if I were you, I'd think it a wise precaution.'

'But you're not me, so how do *you* feel?'

She told him frankly in two caustic words, and he laughed.

'Do you forgive me?' he asked.

'Maybe,' she offered, curving a smile. 'We'll have to see.'

'In the meantime, shall we eat?' he suggested.

As he spoke, Luca teased her lips with a slice of ripe peach, and one thing led to another. Kisses had never been so sweet and delicious as two people shared one slice of peach.

When he sucked peach juice from her mouth she felt a corresponding tug down low in her belly. Then he found the fastening on her gown. Her emotions were all over the place. How could life be so cruel as to allow them to meet, when she was patently un-suited to romancing a prince?

'Hey,' Luca whispered, his lips very close to her mouth, 'anyone would think you were distracted.'

'I am,' she admitted, gasping as he found her nipples through her dress and began to tease them. 'Please stop,' she begged, laughing and moaning with pleasure all at one and the same time.

'You're very sensitive there,' he approved. 'What about here?'

She sucked in a breath as his hand began to work between her legs. Using just his thumb at first, he rubbed gently, but persuasively until his forefinger took over using a more direct approach.

'You know I can't hold on,' she wailed.

'Can't you?'

He sounded so matter-of-fact as he continued to work his magic. 'Relax and open your legs a little more for me,' he instructed.

Obedience was vital and she did so immediately, and was instantly rewarded with the most powerful release yet. It was a long time later when she was finally able to speak, but before she could say anything he began to touch her again. And now it was impossible to concentrate on anything else.

When the waves of her next climax subsided, there was something she had to say.

'I've thought of a way to pay you back.'

'You have? When did I give you the chance to think about that?'

'Earlier,' she chastised softly, 'while I was getting ready for tonight. I thought I could write something for your tourist board to promote Madlena. Advertise the country and its assets.'

She didn't know if she was pleased or not when Luca paused and lifted his head to tell her he thought it a very good idea.

'Well, thank you, kind sir.'

'You're welcome. Now, please allow me to enjoy the rest of my supper...'

CHAPTER ELEVEN

As Samia parted her lips in surprise, he drove his mouth down on hers. She tasted of milk and honey, and it was harder by the minute to remember this was leading to a marriage of convenience. Samia didn't know that yet, although the arrangements were already well under way in Madlena. Meanwhile, her capacity for pleasure seemed endless, which pleased him, and boded well for his scheme.

'Let's go,' he murmured as he soothed her down again and then helped her straighten her dress.

'Yes,' she whispered as he lifted her into his arms.

Her gown was little more than a wisp of material, but even that was a barrier to Samia's lithe and eager body. He wanted nothing more than to rip it off, but was forced to curb the impulse as they crossed the public part of his yacht. Once they were enclosed in opulent silence out of public view, he shifted her position to kiss her, while she clung to him with fingertips made of steel. 'Bed, now,' he growled.

'Or even sooner,' she whispered as he dipped his head to kiss her again. 'Can your crew spare you?'

'I've sorted the problem. They just have to check the sails. This is the real emergency.'

She laughed as he strode on to his stateroom. Shouldering the door, he carried her in. Kicking it closed behind them, he took her zip down and sloughed the dress from her shoulders. 'Step out of it,' he said softly. 'Please,' he added huskily when she gave him a challenging look.

He was beyond impatient to feel her soft warmth yielding beneath him, but willed himself to remain calm. His reward was seeing the need on her face as her shoulders relaxed. She was barefoot and beautiful, and now completely naked; it was Samia's turn to challenge him. 'Undress,' she ordered.

They faced each other. 'You take them off,' he invited. Holding his arms out at his side, he waited. She hesitated a couple of seconds as her desire to strip him warred with a woman who'd been cruelly robbed of enjoying union with a man by her bully of an ex. His will to protect her surged again, even stronger than before.

With no idea of the forces she was unleashing, she began in true Samia style with his belt buckle. 'Stop. This is not the way things should be.'

'How should they be?'

She looked so bewildered, he brought her into his arms. 'Like this,' he said. Kissing her gently, he set her down on the bed. Everything had been racing towards an inevitable conclusion, but suddenly she wrapped her arms around her naked chest and crossed her legs for good measure, hiding her face in her knees. He had never seen a sadder picture. 'If you've changed your mind...' easing his neck, he shrugged '...there's nothing wrong with that. You're frightened. I get it.'

'A little,' she admitted in a small voice.

At that moment, he would have liked to take the individual responsible for doing this to her by the scruff of his neck and bring him to his knees in front of Samia to beg for her forgiveness. 'Did he hurt you very badly?'

'Yes.'

He could barely hear her. 'Every time?'

'Every time,' she confirmed in the faintest of voices.

Gritting his teeth, he lay down beside her and gathered her into his arms. Compared to this, his turmoil was nothing. His emotions had been battered? Not in comparison to Samia's. Any move he made now would feel like a violation. He had to re-evaluate everything.

'Luca?'

'Don't. Don't look at me like that. There's no cause for you to be embarrassed.'

'I've done nothing wrong?' she suggested with a sad little twist of her mouth. 'You must be wondering if you can trust anything I say.'

'No. I believe you.'

'I was running away from his thugs when I blundered into that bar,' she said softly. He stilled, knowing she needed to have someone listen to her. 'He's on his honeymoon with his new young wife, having left instructions to make sure I had a good time too. The only difference is that a good time for me in his eyes is as much pain and suffering as he can inflict. And anyone I turn to will receive the same treatment.' She shook her head in despair and her eyes were stricken as they stared into his. 'I've put you in danger, but I was desperate. I wasn't thinking—'

'You were thinking,' he insisted. 'You needed to get away. And you've put no one in danger, least of all me.'

'He texted me the details of how he'd like to see me beaten up,' she continued, staring blindly into some scene of horror. 'He said I'd never find a hole small enough to hide in.'

Nice, he thought, grinding his jaw. What type of moron did that to a woman, to anyone? Remaining silent, he let Samia talk. This was therapy for a wounded mind. Her profession was immaterial. All he cared about was the well-being of his bride.

'He could never let go of anything he'd once owned,' she was saying, almost as if speaking to herself. 'Goodness knew, I had enough opportunity to learn that while we were together, but I was blind to it, thinking only that I'd lost my mother and now I had to save my father. I left when my father went to prison where my ex couldn't harm him. I know my father wasn't totally blameless, but he was weak, and that monster took advantage of him. I thought I could protect him, but I was wrong.'

'How were you supposed to stand up to a bully

and protect your father, when you could hardly protect yourself?'

'I didn't think. I just knew I had to help him, and I tried.'

'You did your best,' he reassured her, 'and that's all any of us can do.'

'Then, you came along, and yes, while I genuinely didn't know who you were at first, I did see an opportunity to figure out my next move while I was safely away at sea on your yacht.'

He let the silence hang, and then he said, 'Thank you for your honesty. And, for the record? Not all men are the same.'

Relaxing a little, she looked into his eyes. 'I know that now.'

Standing up, he covered her with the sheet and tucked her in, so every inch of her body was covered. He couldn't bear to see her looking so vulnerable. She had nothing to apologise for. It was her ex-husband who should hang his head in shame. Samia was a survivor, and had proved this time and time again. 'I think we both need to take a few deep breaths and step back,' he said.

'What if I don't want to?' she whispered.

When he studied her face, he saw the same appeal that stabbed his heart each time he looked at her. Would this feeling vanish in time, or was it something to build on?

'You're welcome to sleep here,' he told her. 'I'll take a guest suite.'

'Must you?' She held out her hand to him.

'Yes. But first I have a question to ask you.'

'Go on…'

'Marry me.'

'I'm sorry?'

'Marry me. I'll keep you safe, and you'll be doing me a favour.'

Blood drained from her face. 'No,' she told him in a shocked voice.

'No?'

'Do you seriously think I would leave one disaster behind only to walk blindly into another?'

'It would be a sensible arrangement.'

'Sensible?' Her expression turned from shock to anger. 'Is that all I am to you? A convenience? I almost believed you.' Her voice broke. Shooting up in bed, she quickly covered herself again, remembering she was naked. 'I think you'd better leave.'

'My room?'

'All right. I'll leave.' Grabbing the sheet, she stumbled out of bed. He reached out to steady her. She knocked his hand away. 'Don't touch me! Don't even look at me! I'll never forgive you for this!'

Throwing his head back, he roared in agony as she left, slamming the door behind her. To say this situation was new to him would be putting it mildly. If he wanted to keep Samia on side, he'd have to act fast, or he might just lose the best thing that had ever happened to him.

She took a shower, which gave her the chance to re-flect on Luca's proposal. It was hard to believe he was serious. How could he be? Why choose her? Did he think her so malleable and such a fool that she would marry simply for advantage? Was that what people did in royal circles? Maybe, but it would never be enough for her. But she refused to hide away here. She would confront him. She'd tried and failed to save her father, but she would not fail this test. This was the new Samia. Luca might wield all the power in the world, but she would stand up to him.

She'd calmed down a little by the time she got dressed, and had accepted that family was every-thing, for her and for Luca, and, as far as he was con-cerned, Madlena was his family, and he would do anything to safeguard his people, which was where she came in. The Pirate Prince clearly needed a bride to reassure the citizens of Madlena that he was bringing them peace and optimism, not tur-moil and uncertainty. But surely he must have a list of princesses waiting with bated breath for his call? Madlena might be small, but it was a fabulously wealthy little island since his parents had arrived at the brilliant solution of turning it into a tax haven. She could only imagine the long line of hopefuls vying for a slice of that.

Perhaps he'd been looking for something more than an avaricious princess?

But I'm no one. Why choose me? What have I got to offer? If I were choosing a bride for Luca...

Yes?

She couldn't even bear to think about it. Which was ridiculous, remembering their latest encounter. It was time to find out exactly what was going on—in her head as well as his.

Still reeling from Samia's refusal, Luca was ready to concede that he could have put it better, or maybe chosen a better moment, but he was a plain-speaking man.

Leaving the shower with a towel wrapped around his waist, he used another to towel dry his hair vigorously before raking it with impatient fingers. He had always wanted everything yesterday.

She had come back?

He stilled as Samia entered the room wearing a plush robe she'd thrown on, and had belted carelessly in her rush to get back.

To him?

Maybe not, he thought dazedly as she launched into a tirade. *Guilty on all counts*, he mused. She went on to list all the reasons why she couldn't marry him.

'I'm a divorcee. My father's in prison.'

'He was convicted of fraud. Am I right?'

'You've read his file, I imagine?'

'I have,' he confirmed. 'Further investigation proved that the mysterious funds in your father's bank account lead straight back to your ex.'

'Everyone knows that. They were to pay off his gambling debts.'

'No. He had already paid those off.'

'What?'

This new information stripped away her battling

front, replacing it with an expression of hope so intense it was almost painful to see. 'The funds that put your father in prison were added to his account at a later date. It's my belief he was set up, and I intend to prove it.'

'Can you do that?'

'My lawyers can. They seem quite confident.'

'If you could do that, I—'

Never one to miss an opportunity, he suggested, 'You'd marry me?'

'I didn't say that,' she fired back.

'I'm not trying to blackmail you with empty promises. My lawyers are working on your father's case as we speak and whatever answer you give to my proposal, they will continue to work until he's free. That's all I can say at this moment. I can't do anything about your mother's death, and I regret that more than you know. The damage done by your ex-husband was a tsunami that took down everything in its wake. Except you,' he stated levelly.

'Don't do this,' she said, covering her face with her hands. 'I need time to think.'

'You can have all the time in the world—if you make a decision today.'

Choosing to ignore the joke, she raised angry eyes to his. 'You can't heal everything with sheer force of will.'

'But I can try.'

She seemed to accept this, although a lot of seconds ticked by before she started speaking again, and by then she was reflective. 'I don't want to do anything without careful consideration first. My mother always said I rushed into things, but then the real world was a mystery to her, and she couldn't appreciate that sometimes opportunities had to be seized. She was never fitted for enduring reality. Raised in a cocoon of wealth and privilege, she expected that to continue for the rest of her life. I just wish I could have talked to her, to prove how many good things there are away from top show and empty possessions, and all the opportunities she was missing.'

'Some people just don't want to hear the truth. You can't blame yourself for that.'

There was another long silence, and then she admitted, 'I didn't expect you to be so understanding.'

'I'm not. I'm an impatient man with a country to reassure. I'm not proud of my motives, but I ask you to understand them.' Marrying to seal a deal that benefited both parties made perfect sense to him.

'This is marriage we're talking about,' she confirmed.

'Of course.'

'I could give you another list of reasons why I can't marry you.'

'But none of them would make sense.'

'To you, maybe.'

'I don't understand what's stopping you.'

'Your arrogance? Your sense of entitlement? Your assumption that you only have to speak and I will jump?'

'Am I allowed to voice a defence?'

Her jaw worked as she stared at him. 'Here,' she said, tossing him a robe. 'Put this on. You're far too distracting.' No one had ever complained before. 'If this is a serious proposal of marriage, I can only assume you have a touch of sunstroke, and should rest.'

'I can assure you I'm sound in mind as well as body.'

'I can see that,' she agreed, narrowing her eyes.

He'd in no way won her over yet, or made up for his crass proposal, but, catching the robe one-handed, he shrugged it on as they exchanged a searing look.

CHAPTER TWELVE

MUSCLES RIPPLING, his wild hair even wilder than ever following some rough attention with a towel, Luca was nothing short of magnificent. She knew he was mocking her with that smouldering look, but he could afford to take chances. She couldn't, and that was the difference between them. The Pirate Prince was taking one last throw of the dice—and, quite amazingly, it was in her direction—before he settled down to rule Madlena. All this talk of marrying him… What was she to make of it? It wasn't easy to think straight in the face of so much potent male attraction, which he knew. But she would think straight. She was the most unsuitable bride he could have picked. Even forgetting her past, she had no skills in the bedroom, and a rebellious soul, that, now it was free, wouldn't tolerate restrictions made by any man. She couldn't think of a worse choice off the top of her head.

'If you're looking for a bride to inspire confidence in your people, I don't think I'm your gal.'

'I disagree,' he said firmly.

'You would. But there's something else.'

'Go on,' he prompted, angling a chin that needed a good close shave.

'I don't want to be a princess.'

'Because you like your life the way it is? The notion of jewels and status, and the best seats at every event, travel by private jet wearing fancy clothes, and people bowing and scraping for no better reason than you have a meaningless prefix before your name—none of that appeals to you?'

'No. It doesn't,' she agreed.

'Greeting dignitaries you can't stand?'

'Horrible.'

'What about meeting those who need your support?'

'Well, that's different,' she said as if this were obvious. 'Of course I'd do everything I could to help, if I were in a position to do so.'

'It might surprise you to know I feel exactly the same. I'll do whatever it takes to serve my people and to help build my country into a flag bearer for fairness and equality, but when it comes to endless banquets and court affairs, I'm going to need someone to prod me to make sure I stay awake.'

'And that's my job?' she queried, shooting him a scathing look.

'You can always plead a headache and I'll ask someone else to do it.'

'This isn't a joke, Luca. Seriously. Who wants to be royal? No privacy, no comments you can trust won't be repeated, guarding everything you say while you're surrounded by sycophants pretending to be your friend? I've always pitied those who carry that burden, and have never wished to join them. Don't forget I've had my fifteen minutes of fame—infamy, in my case—and it was a hideous experience.'

'Because you were unhappy, and had no one to support you,' Luca countered firmly.

He was right, but how could she pretend to be something she was not, and could never be? 'I can't just brush my past under the carpet and become a saintly princess.'

'Heaven forbid! Brushing anything under the carpet is the last thing I'd want you to do. You can build on your past experiences, and I'd want you to bring them to bear on everything you do. In that way, you can use them to help others. I've seen you interact with my crew. I've felt your natural warmth and observed how well you relate to everyone. I can't think of a better endorsement for a princess than people taking you to their hearts. I imagine that's the quality that made you such a successful journalist, until your column was corrupted by someone no one, not even you, could control.'

Because my ex owned the newspaper, she reflected ruefully, *as you rule Madlena. Am I heading for Groundhog Day?*

'You're intuitive and empathetic,' Luca continued, 'which draws people to you. I believe that quality would in time make you a much-loved Princess of Madlena.'

'You *are* serious about this marriage proposal,'

she said through lips that felt numb and stiff as they formed words she found it impossible to get her head around.

'Of course I am,' Luca insisted. 'I would hardly joke about something like that. All I ask is that you commit to a certain period of time for our marriage— say five years. That should be enough to reassure my people that I can be the Prince they need. You'd have all the freedom you wanted during that time—'

'Let me stop you there,' she rapped out, grim-faced. 'You're putting boundaries on the duration of your marriage?'

'Our marriage,' he emphasised with a look as steely as hers. 'I thought that was what you would want. You don't want to be tied to me for ever.'

Luca was as damaged as she was, Samia reflected as he went on, 'We would need to remain married long enough to reassure my people that I intend to be the stable leader they hope for. Five years should do it.'

'And when those five years are up, I pack my bags and leave to write a book? I'd make millions telling our story, and, of course, I'd live happily ever after.'

'A simple clause in the marriage contract should prevent the writing of a tell-all book,' Luca reflected out loud.

'You expect me to stick around for five years, busying myself by putting my name to worthy causes, and never getting my hands dirty, of course?'

'Now you're being sarcastic,' he observed, 'and

I thought better of you. I would never stop you taking a proper role in any cause you felt drawn to.'

'How good of you,' she said sweetly. 'And when I return to the real world—with a pension, presumably, so I never have to work another day in my life—what then? I wear a gag and take up tatting?'

'That won't be necessary,' Luca said stiffly. 'We'll visit the lawyers again and sign the required prenup—'

'Excuse me?' she cut in. '*Who* will sign the prenup?'

'Why, you, of course,' Luca confirmed.

'Of course,' Samia agreed caustically. 'I'd be only too pleased to protect you in every way I can.'

'I knew you'd see sense eventually.'

'*Sense?*' she snarled. 'Have you been indulging yourself sailing around the world for so long you've lost touch completely with reality? In my world, women work and raise families, build homes that are warm and loving sanctuaries, care for others, and improve themselves, all at one and the same time. Not at any point do they sit back and let a man take the helm.'

'I think you misunderstand me.'

'I think I've got a perfect grasp of the situation. You command and I obey.'

'It wouldn't be like that.'

'And my guarantee?'

'Do you need it spelled out?'

'Yes. I think I do. If you have a contract for me to sign, then I'll have one for you as well.'

'So, that's a yes to my proposal, then?'

She had to stop her jaw dropping to the floor at his sheer audacity. This was the Pirate Prince at full throttle, doing what he did best, which was to cut a swathe through all objections. Luca needed her to say yes, and he wasn't too bothered about the form in which her agreement came.

'At no point do you find this preposterous?' she demanded.

'No,' he confirmed, looking genuinely bemused. 'Why would I? Perhaps I could have put it better...'

'Perhaps you could,' she agreed.

'I genuinely think this will benefit both of us,' he insisted. 'I don't consider it outlandish in any way. People enter into arranged marriages all the time. If there are enough common factors and sound foundations to build on, there's no reason why a marriage of convenience can't be a success.'

'For five years?'

'Or for whatever term you state. I'm merely suggesting a minimum of five years.'

She really needed to sit down before her legs gave way. This was so far beyond her ken she didn't have a ready answer, just feelings that threatened to overflow and drown her. 'So here's my take on the situation,' she offered with a deceptively mild expression on her face.

'Please,' Luca invited, opening his arms to encourage her, obviously believing that she was on the point of giving in.

'As my first marriage proved, there are no guarantees in life, and mistakes can always be made, but to walk blindly into something twice would be supremely stupid, and I'm not daft.'

'No. You're a very clever woman,' he agreed, 'or I wouldn't be asking the question.'

'I'm also a dreamer, as you've noted, and my dream is to find the right man to marry so I can build a home and raise children, help others—all those points I mentioned before. At no stage of my dream is there a contract stating when it's time to wake up and find everything I care about has gone. You might find this hard to believe, but I still believe in love, and I still value marriage, and if and when I marry again, it will be with total love and commitment, and with no boundaries or contracts to define the terms.'

'But you accept that a second marriage might not work out for you?'

'Of course I do. I have to. There are two people involved, not just me. There are no certainties in life for any of us.'

'Then, what's the difference between our propositions?' Luca demanded, throwing his arms wide with frustration.

'Mine is made with love, while yours is made with a deal in mind.'

'Maybe you expect too much.'

'Maybe I do,' she agreed.

They were both quiet for quite a while, and then he said the one thing she'd been dreading. 'There's something else behind your reluctance, isn't there, Samia?'

She'd been blunt with him so far. She couldn't back down now. 'I'm no good in bed,' she said, staring him straight in the eyes as if daring him to disagree.

'Surely, that's for me to judge?' Luca said quietly.

'I don't care to be judged.'

'Perhaps judged is the wrong expression,' he conceded. 'What I meant was, this would be a new beginning…for both of us.'

She perched on the edge of the bed to give herself a chance to think. Luca was leaning against the wall with his unbelted robe slipping off one shoulder, which exposed the thick column of his neck, and a wealth of impossibly powerful muscle. That wasn't exactly helpful when it came to clear thinking.

She took her time, and then said, 'It isn't wrong not to like sex.'

'Wrong? No,' Luca agreed. 'I just find it impossible to believe you fall into that category.'

He'd neatly sidestepped the marriage question, she noticed, but his remark was due an answer. 'I don't know why you find it so hard to believe.'

Those shoulders eased in a lazy shrug that made her heart thunder. 'I've seen you come apart in my arms,' he murmured, fixing his gaze on her face. 'I've heard you beg for more. I've felt you respond, and I've tasted your passion. I've seen the tiger inside you unleash its claws, and yet now you're asking me to believe you don't enjoy sex. Forgive me if I don't believe you.'

'But what if I can't…?' A dry throat was bad enough. A strangled throat was worse.

'Can't what?' Luca demanded, refusing to let her off the hook.

'What if I can't go the whole way and give you a proper marriage?' The humiliation of giving voice to her fears was so overwhelming, she wasn't sure she could hold back the tears.

'Like every other couple,' Luca responded in a matter-of-fact tone, 'we'll face that hurdle when we come to it.'

'No,' she said decisively. 'You don't understand. I can't—I really can't.'

'Because…?'

'Because I can't face it—'

'Face what? Go on, say it,' he insisted as she pressed her lips together.

'I can't stand penetrative sex,' she blurted. 'There. You've got what you wanted. I've said it. And why are we even discussing this?' she added before Luca had the chance to say a word. 'Why must you torment me, when it's obvious that marriage between us is a ridiculous idea?'

'I don't agree. We can marry, and we will.' He let that fact settle in, and then he added, 'Are there any other issues you'd like to raise?'

A fist maybe? To plant in his arrogant face. Apart from that…?

Feelings exploded inside her.

'Nothing more to say?' he prompted. 'Then, let me reassure you that you can safely leave those concerns to me.'

'Why bother?' she flared. 'There must be countless women gagging for the job of Princess!'

'But none I want,' Luca said flatly. 'I will marry you. And here's why. I need a bride to reassure my people. You say you're unsuitable. Let's think about that. Who could be more fitting to sit on the throne of Madlena than a woman who's suffered, and experienced life on the outside? You've haven't been hiding away in an ivory tower, you've been working. You've coped with your mother's death, and you did everything you could to help your father, while living through a personal trauma. Who better to mould the Pirate Prince into a decent human being than a tried and tested survivor who has come out on the other side, armed with knowledge and experience? Not only are you ready to help my people, you're eager to do it too.'

'So your argument is, I will influence you in a positive way?'

'My argument is that it will look that way.'

'As I thought. Even you have to admit that's hardly persuasive.'

Luca shrugged. 'If you want to pick holes in my argument, neither of us is a suitable candidate for the throne. We're both tainted, but I believe this can work, if we want it to. With our joint experience of the world, we can make the type of difference Madlena needs. Our people will take you to their hearts and I'll join you on that ride. Who can resist a "bad boy turned good" story?'

'Someone who doesn't see the world from your

cynical point of view. You want your people to love you, but you're frightened to give them your heart.'

What chance do I stand? she wondered.

'I'm being realistic,' Luca argued, starting to pace the room. 'Which is what Madlena needs. My brother lived in an ivory tower, where he was aloof and untouchable but adored, because his life was so closely guarded he never appeared to make a mistake. I *want* to get my hands dirty. I want to take risks for the good of my people, and through it all I'm going to be on full view with my bride at my side, taking part in life as a citizen of Madlena. I'll make mistakes. I'm bound to, but I'll do everything I can to put them right, and it's my hope you'll buy into that, because I know you'll be a great asset to the throne.'

'That's a rather cold-blooded assessment.'

'Yes, it is,' Luca admitted frankly. He stopped pacing in front of her. 'I expect the services of a loyal bride with all that that entails, while you get guaranteed safety, along with a life that, I can tell you now, will take all your energy, but that will fully repay you, by fulfilling your every need.'

Every need? She had no expectations of that where the marriage bed was concerned, and even less when it came to some small sign from Luca that one day they might mean more to each other than two parties entering a contract *that made perfect sense.* She was falling for this man, while he'd practically admitted he was incapable of love. This could be her worst dream come true. Perhaps her ex was right. Perhaps she would never be worthy of love. At least, not the type of love she longed for, both to give and receive. She dreamed of a love that had no boundaries, and that spread its light far and wide, and her greatest hope had always been to make that dream a reality.

She had another major niggle too. 'I'm not sure about the *services* of a loyal bride. I would need to know what these services entail.'

Luca's gaze sharpened. 'Before you agree?'

'I haven't decided anything yet.'

'You want me to understand that you bow your head to no man?' Luca suggested.

'Never again,' she confirmed. Her mouth twisted ruefully. 'I tried it once, and look where that got me.'

'Some would say, into a very good place.'

'But not me,' she assured him.

'Let me make this clear. By *services* I mean no scoops in the press, no sudden surprises. I would never stop you writing. I can see the benefits to Madlena. And I would never stop you doing anything you want to do, unless it posed a risk to our country.'

In spite of her doubts, Luca using the phrase '*our* country' gave her pause for thought, and a thrill of anticipation ran through her mind as she considered all the possibilities that weren't connected to wealth or status. If she didn't at least consider his argument, she was being as closed off as her mother. She had to listen and weigh the facts. Only then could she give him her answer.

'Would you want to read everything I wrote and approve it first?' she asked, remembering past shackles. *And then change it?* The words bounced around in her mind. That was her biggest fear. If Luca turned out to be anything like her ex, she really was leaping from the frying pan into the fire.

'If you become Princess of Madlena, I would expect you to have the country's best interests at heart.'

'I would. Don't take that as my answer,' she warned when a flame sparked in Luca's eyes.

'It goes without saying that your ex will never trouble you again,' he added, as set as she was on getting his point across. 'When your father leaves prison—and we have every reason to believe that will be sooner, rather than later—I'll ensure he receives all the help he needs to get back on his feet, as well as a plan going forward. So long as he does nothing to hurt you, he'll always be a welcome guest in our home.'

These offers were wonderful and generous, but Luca had made not one single mention of romance. His suggestion remained a cold-blooded arrangement to benefit both of them. It was hard to argue with a single word he'd said, but that didn't stop her heart aching for something it couldn't have. *Something I obviously don't deserve.* He'd been wholly objective when he laid out the details of their contract, which made his promise to 'sort out her problem' more terrifying than exciting. Could he do that? Could anyone? What if she failed utterly in bed, or recoiled as she had in the past?

Worse. What if she proved to be frigid, as her ex had insisted she was?

And yet... And yet...

Family was everything, and how could she help her father if she didn't have a job, or even a home to go back to? He'd always been weak and easily influenced. Wouldn't it be better for him to be influenced by strong people with good intentions? Could she deny him that chance? She could provide him with all the love in the world when he came out of prison, but nights were cold, and his belly would be empty without the practical support Luca had offered. Wasn't this one thing she could do for her mother, who must have loved her father at some point? Shouldn't she do everything she could to set her father back on his feet?

CHAPTER THIRTEEN

SHE QUICKLY GATHERED her wits. Helping her father was the one unselfish act she could accept as a reason for marrying Luca.

Hadn't she done that once before? What made him different?

She'd learned from past mistakes, and would put safeguards in place. Luca wasn't her ex-husband, but a man of principle. His reputation might be colourful, but she'd seen first-hand his determination to change. Marriage was all part of that long road to redemption, and, though theirs would be a cold-blooded marriage, he was right in saying they both had something to gain from it. But when they went to the lawyers she would not remain silent. There was more than money at stake. There was her father's future, and her dreams at stake.

So I've made my decision?

Her mind was still in turmoil. She might be able to do some good as Princess of Madlena... She'd have a platform, if nothing else... But first, Luca had to hear her conditions. 'I can't take this further until you hear my requests.'

She had thought he might object, but now realised she should have expected the flare of triumph in his eyes. 'I'm keen to hear your views,' he said.

'I'll continue writing, and you can't censor my work in any way.'

'That's easy to agree,' he confirmed.

'I'd be free to travel?'

'It isn't my intention to cage you. You seem distracted?' he observed when she fell silent.

'*If* I agree to your suggestion—and I'm nowhere near close to that yet—I would need to undertake a real, practical role. I could never agree to being a puppet princess, wheeled out now and then for the sake of appearances.'

Luca laughed, and as he threw his head back, making his thick, wavy hair catch on his stubble, she almost weakened.

'I'm sorry,' he said, curbing his laughter with obvious difficulty. 'I realise this isn't the best time for humour, but you in the role of meek, obedient wife? I'm sorry, but that's a stretch too far. And I don't want that,' he insisted. 'I need challenge. I expect you to espouse causes and fight for them tooth and claw. Being "wheeled out," as you put it, on state occasions, is a little harder to imagine. I'll have to rely on your better nature to oblige me when it comes to that. I'd be wasting your talents if all you did was to sit dumbly at my side. I'm hoping you would want to use your royal role for the good of the people.'

'But—'

'There's something else?' he queried when she broke off.

'Yes,' she admitted.

'Go on,' he prompted.

'If I'm hopeless in…'

'In bed?' he supplied.

'If I can't… If I really can't stand it…'

'I assume we're talking about sex?'

Swallowing convulsively, she nodded her head.

'Remember, I do know a little about you.' His lips tugged fractionally, though not in a mocking smile, but with understanding.

They had very few secrets left when it came to her physical responses, she accepted. It was just that life-changing next step she dreaded.

"You can stop looking so worried. We won't sleep together until our wedding night, by which time you will be—'

Ready?' she whispered. It was more question than a statement.

Luca shrugged.

Her imagination raced ahead. When it came to wanting him there was no problem. The comfort of his arms around her, and the pleasure of his touch— those were wonderful. But the pain she associated with penetrative sex—

Sucking in a great shuddering breath, she knew for certain that she would never be ready for that.

Crossing the room in a couple of strides, he took Samia in his arms. There could never be sufficient punishment for what that bully had done to this woman. She couldn't accept that a man could be kind? What kind of legacy was that? His negotiations were still under way, but the offer of physical warmth had no conditions. And she was in no hurry to break away, he noticed. 'You'll be fine,' he soothed. 'You'll make the right decision. I won't say anything more, or try to influence you.'

She laughed softly, her voice muffled against his chest. 'You already have influenced me. I tried to fight you, and found I don't want to. Can we just be friends?'

Samia was naked beneath the robe, her arousal plain to see. Her nipples thrust imperatively against the robe, and he guessed the rest of her body would be equally receptive.

'Don't you want me?' she asked. 'Or are you just playing me to get what you want?

Even he wasn't entirely sure about his motives, but he did know he wanted her. 'I want you,' he confirmed as he pulled away. 'But we're going to wait until our wedding night.'

'You're very confident,' she whispered.

'Yes. I am.'

CHAPTER FOURTEEN

HE MET SAMIA again at breakfast the next morn-ing, beneath an awning on deck where an exqui-sitely dressed dining table with a crisp white damask cloth and napkins, crystal glasses, delicate porcelain plates and silver cutlery was a setting fit for a prin-cess. A role Samia played with consummate ease, and unassuming elegance, he noted as a steward di-rected her to the chair next to his.

Rising from his place, he rose and stood until she was comfortably seated, then settled himself and eased back in his seat. 'I trust you slept well?'

'I trust you did?' she countered.

He hadn't had a moment's sleep. He'd been too busy making arrangements. The first of these would come to fruition in about half an hour.

'You look refreshed,' he commented. She took his breath away. 'I see you've been raiding the clos-ets again?'

'No point in being coy about it,' she explained with her normal forthrightness, flicking her still-damp hair out of the way. 'I don't have any other clothes with me.'

'I have to say, those simple sundresses look beautiful on you.'

'Someone has very good taste,' she observed dryly. 'And before you ask, I wasn't fishing for information on who that might be.'

'Yes, you were.' It pleased him to think she might be jealous.

'Her loss is my gain.'

Samia's pointed stare reminded him of an opponent in the ring. This tussle wasn't over yet—it was only just beginning. *And it might have a lifetime to run.*

He brushed the thought away as a steward intervened at just the right moment with coffee. Things would never be easy between him and Samia, but that was half the stimulating fun of it. She wasn't exactly immune to him, either, he thought as she moistened her lips and looked away.

'So,' he probed, 'is the Pirate Prince about to become a reformed character?'

'I would have thought that was up to you.'

'My question requires an answer.'

'I haven't decided yet.'

'Then, you should. Time is running out…' As he spoke, they both turned in the direction of an approaching helicopter.

'Visitors?' she said. Shielding her eyes with her hand, she stared up into the harsh early morning light.

'Heralding the start of a day devoted entirely to your pleasure,' he explained.

'I don't understand.' She frowned.

'There's nothing *to* understand. The question is simple. I asked you to be my bride. I'm asking you again—formally asking, this time—and I need your answer now.'

'*Now?* You mean, right now?'

'Right now,' he confirmed.

He was glad he'd chosen an emerald engagement ring to match her eyes. It was the perfect choice. The royal jeweller had excelled herself with a Herculean effort, working through the night to create what Luca considered to be the most beautiful jewel he'd ever seen, and then having it transported by launch at dead of night.

'What's this?' Samia exclaimed as he produced the midnight-blue velvet box from the breast pocket of his shirt.

'A priceless gem, made with consummate skill and the utmost devotion by a world-renowned jeweller in Madlena.'

If he had been the type of man to puff himself up, he would have puffed at that moment, so proud was he of the craftspeople of Madlena. He was confident that Samia would be blown away. He had seen many fabulous pieces of jewellery in his time, but nothing to compare with the clarity, colour and cut of the gemstone currently residing in the palm of his hand. 'Try it on,' he invited.

'Really?' As she pulled her head back it was clear she didn't know whether to laugh or smile. 'May I?'

'Of course,' She should get used to such things.

She took the ring from his hand and stared at it in wonder as a child might on Christmas morning after picking something choice out of a stocking. The priceless stone glowed green like the heart of a rainforest, while the sizeable diamonds surrounding it flashed like Arctic fire. As she held it up to the light, she laughed. 'It looks like green ice.' But then she handed it back to him. 'What a whopper,' she remarked. 'My granny would love it. Oh, I'm sorry,' she blurted, realising she might have caused offence. 'I mean, the ring is absolutely gorgeous, but just not for me.'

The helicopter hovered over them like a noisy black cloud determined to rain on his parade. Denied further conversation, he could only sit and seethe in response to Samia's unexpected reaction to the ring he had chosen with such care, as its powerful engines screamed overhead. His affront would have to wait, he concluded as the pilot lined up for a pinprick perfect landing on the *Black Diamond*'s helipad. He had more pressing matters to attend to now. Prince Luca Fortebracci wasn't noted for indecision and he saw no reason for their marriage to be delayed any longer.

'Shall I stay here while you greet your guests?' Samia enquired as the engines quietened to an agitated purr. 'The ring's beautiful—honestly, it is,' she added, seeing his closed expression. 'I hope you're not too offended by what I said? I realise now you probably designed it—and with me in mind.'

'Who else?' he gritted out.

'If I decide to marry anyone, it won't be the ring that seals the deal,' she assured him. 'Love and trust would be enough for me.'

'After everything you've been through?' he queried sceptically.

'Expensive jewellery wouldn't change any of that, and it certainly can't be a deciding factor in whether or not I accept your proposal. I always think a plain gold or platinum band is all that's needed to reflect a circle of love.'

'That's your romantic side speaking for you.'

'Good,' she said. 'It's nice to know I can still rustle up a few romantic feelings after going ten rounds in the ring, so to speak.' She chuckled at her own expense. 'Wasn't it you who said that not all men are the same? Well, not all women are the same, either, and for me it's what's in the heart, not on the finger, that counts.'

It was hard to be offended when Samia's smile was so genuine it lit up her eyes, making them more like precious gems than the ring in the box he was gripping so tightly it threatened to dent. Putting it back in his pocket, he leaned over to plant his fists on the table. 'Samia,' he said quietly, 'I really do need your answer now. Will you marry me?' As he asked the question the helicopter engines were switched off, and the abrupt silence made him appear to shout.

'I will!' she shouted back, springing to her feet.

He was so shocked by her sudden acquiescence that he barely heard her add, 'I guess I'll get used to the idea eventually—if you give me enough time...'

'There is no time,' he said briskly. 'We'll be docking in Madlena tomorrow morning, and my intention is to arrive with a bride.'

'I'm sorry?' Samia demanded. 'At the risk of sounding like a complete dimwit, who exactly is this bride going to be?'

'The captain of my *floating office block* will marry us tonight. I trust that is acceptable?'

Her mouth worked but she said nothing. Luca took the chance to fill the sudden silence with essential information. 'I will go and greet our guests— hairdresser, make-up artist, fashion designers, and a seamstress to make any necessary alterations to your wedding gown and, of course, my indispensable PA, Domenico, who will direct events. Three of them will act as our witnesses, and then the helicopter will return them to shore, while you and I discuss our future over a candlelit dinner before retiring to our marriage bed.'

Ice gathered in the pit of her stomach. 'I... I thought I would have longer to get used to the idea before we were actually married.'

'Think again.'

It seemed that Luca was done with waiting.

* * *

Numb with shock, Samia was in a state of complete unreality as she allowed herself to be ushered back to her stateroom by an immaculately groomed gentleman who introduced himself as Domenico. Luca's PA wouldn't have looked out of place behind a mahogany and glass counter in Savile Row, but he seemed kind, and funny, and was trying very hard to put her at ease. She'd need something, she reflected as he hustled her away. Everything was happening so quickly she had barely had a chance to breathe.

Left alone to bathe for a scant ten minutes, she exited the bathroom in a robe, ready to be primped and preened by beauticians, who then handed her over to the charge of a hairdresser who, it had to be said, worked wonders with her wilful hair. Though so many pins were required to hold up the heavy mass of gleaming curls, they stuck into her scalp like vindictive darts, reminding her of a lifetime of discomfort ahead. Her thighs tingled as she tensed them. High-heeled shoes and tiaras would be the least of that discomfort. She couldn't deny Luca the physical side of marriage for ever.

'There will be photographers,' Domenico explained as he twitched the yards of filmy fabric that comprised her gown until it obeyed his smallest command. 'I hope you like the dresses I chose for you to try on. Signor Luca insisted they should be understated, or he warned you might consign them to Davy Jones's locker.'

'Toss this in the sea?' Samia queried on a disbelieving breath as she ran her hands down the front of the exquisite gown she and Domenic had finally decided on. 'Never.'

In a flattering shade of ivory, the bridal gown was a dream of a dress, composed of the softest, finest chiffon that moulded her figure like a second skin. It didn't constrict, or stop her leaning over in case she revealed more than she intended.

'I can't believe you've second-guessed my taste like this.'

'That credit goes to Prince Luca,' Domenico informed her as she twizzled around in front of the mirror in an attempt to see the gown from every angle.

'Clothing the body of a beautiful woman requires a very different approach to that of someone who only seeks to impress. Building on Prince Luca's recommendations, I saw instantly that you are a free spirit, but strong, which made my vision for you something that floated as you stamped your mark on the world.'

She laughed. 'You make me sound formidable.'

'Time will tell,' Domenico observed with a sniff. 'The main thing now is that you like it. Prince Luca trusts me, and in this instance with his most important project yet.'

Samia frowned. 'I'm not sure I like being described as a project.'

Taking hold of her shoulders in a light grip, Domenico held her at arm's length. 'Are you sure about this?' he asked with an appraising stare.

'Can anyone be sure about anything?'

'That is not an answer. I can see that Prince Luca has plenty to gain by marrying you, but what do you get out of it? He has no idea when it comes to romance. I imagine he attempted to woo you with some vulgar display of extravagance?'

'Well, I wouldn't call it that, but—'

'It's only because he doesn't know any better. Prince Luca chose to make his home in a barracks, and no doubt imagined that a grand gesture was required when it came to his bride. Don't be too hard on him. He's a good man, and if anyone can soften him, I believe that person is you.'

'A snap judgement?' she suggested.

'That's why he keeps me at his side. I haven't been wrong yet,' Domenico told her.

'I only wish I had your confidence.'

'You should. You're beautiful, and you look stunning in this gown, but, more important than that, you have a good heart and a brave spirit. I've done my investigating too.'

'It seems we're all sleuths around here.'

Domenico smiled warmly. 'Turn around and take another look at yourself in the mirror, and then tell me that you're not a princess.'

She did as Domenico suggested, and found herself looking at a stranger who seemed so poised. The stranger was exquisitely dressed, as if she had stepped out of the pages of one of the fairy tales

Samia's mother used to read when Samia was a little girl.

If only her mother had lived to see this day...

Straightening her spine, she lifted her chin. Her beloved mother was gone. She couldn't change that, but she could remember one of the last things her mother had said, which was, the best way to cope with loss was for the survivor to continue playing the role she always had. *Be my daughter. Make me proud. Hold on to that, because then you'll have a purpose that will help you climb out of the dark into the light.* That was what she would do. This was not a time for doubt, but a time to remember she had a father to care for and a life to live. And why not this life? She would embrace the role of Princess wholeheartedly as she did everything else. She'd only ever wanted to help and love and give, and now she had that chance. This new life would be like her column, where her purpose had been to find solutions for other people's problems and make things right, and now she could do that for Luca and his subjects.

'Just your veil now...'

She realised Domenico was still standing there patiently as he waited for her to come out of her temporary trance. He needed to finish helping her dress, and had a band of fresh flowers resting on his perfectly manicured hand, and a foam of twinkling tulle draped across his arm. 'Sorry to keep you waiting,' she apologised with a smile. 'Daydreaming is a terrible habit of mine, and I can't seem to shake it.'

'You should never do so,' Domenico insisted.

'Without dreams, what are we? Without them we'd never strive.'

'Agreed,' she said, 'but must I wear a veil? It hardly seems appropriate under these circumstances, and I'd rather leave my hair free. I'm not even sure I can keep a veil on if we go on deck. Knowing my luck, it will probably blow away.'

'I'd say your luck is about to change for the better.'

'Luca!' At the sound of his voice, she swung around in surprise.

'You don't have to do anything you don't want to do,' he confirmed. 'Thank you, Domenico,' he added pleasantly. 'You can leave us now.'

Breath hitched in Samia's throat as she looked at the man she was about to marry. His hair was still damp from the shower, and his stubble was growing rapidly in spite of a recent shave. Luca Fortebracci was any woman's dream. Tanned, ruggedly good-looking, and built like a gladiator, he was a most imposing sight, a prince amongst men in every sense of the word. In a crisp white shirt and a beautifully tailored pale linen suit, he was impossibly good-looking. So how could she hesitate?

Because she was the girl from nowhere, whose only talent lay with words. And yet, the fact that this man was determined to rush her into this marriage seemed more of a blessing than a curse.

CHAPTER FIFTEEN

'YOU LOOK BEAUTIFUL,' Luca murmured as he held her gaze.

And breathe, she instructed herself firmly as he stopped in front of her—though a disappointingly 'sensible' distance away, as her old headmistress might have said. There were documents in his hand, she registered belatedly. It was time to come out of her dazzled trance and face reality.

'I can't believe this is happening.'

'Rest assured, it is, and to mark the occasion, there are some documents for you to sign.'

To seal our deal, she thought as her happiness dropped away. And why was she surprised, when she had always known what she was getting into? She couldn't think of a single useful thing to say as her heart squeezed tight. If it had been china, it might have shattered into tiny pieces. Luckily for her, she was made of sterner stuff. 'Thank you,' she said, reaching for the papers. 'I'll read them through.'

As she closed her fingers around the stiff vellum, Luca maintained his grip so they were joined by the sheaf of legal papers. Better than nothing, she reflected as they stared into each other's eyes.

'My legal team has already been in discussion with your father, and all things are settled, though he has made one request that, I must admit, I hadn't anticipated.'

'Oh?' She was still shuffling the cards in her brain, only to have this curveball thrown into the mix. 'I'm surprised you didn't tell me sooner.'

'I've only just found out, and time is of the essence.'

'What is the request?' she pressed, fearing the worst, and hoping her father hadn't asked Luca's team for money.

Releasing his end of the legal papers, Luca stepped back to explain. 'He's extremely happy for you, and glad things have worked out. He wants to reassure you that he's keen to leave his old life behind, and his only wish is to live in the Highlands as a crofter where he once owned some land.'

Until her ex stole it from him, Samia remembered unhappily.

'This is a fortunate turn of events,' Luca assured her, 'as I own an estate in Scotland.' Of course he did, she thought incredulously, happily, fondly. 'My gamekeeper and his team are the best of men, and would like to help your father. I hope that's a satisfactory conclusion to your concern?'

It was so much to take in she could only nod her head dumbly. 'How can I ever thank you?' she said hoarsely at last.

A flicker of humour flared in Luca's eyes. 'By marrying me?' he suggested.

The helicopter brought another captain on board. His colleague would marry them, Luca explained when he left Samia reading the documents he'd brought to her stateroom as proof of his intentions. She impressed him by handing over her own document of wishes and reassurances, which she asked him to sign. These were hastily written, not by a legal team, as his were, with endless checks and balances throughout, but emotional, and small. She expected so little. Her bar was set very low, which made him want to give her the world. It was a shame that things had to be so calculated and rushed like this, but he didn't want to risk her backing out once she got to Madlena. After a harsh start in life, stumbling from one crisis to the next as she attempted to shore up her parents' chaotic existence, Samia deserved a proper courtship, and a man who could offer both his undivided attention and unstinting devotion. That man was not Luca. He had a country to put first, a reputation to salvage, and a brother he still mourned. Slim pickings for a bride whose imagination took her on endless flights of fancy, and, in spite of his devotion to duty, he only wished he could offer her more.

Domenico gave her away. They'd formed a bond in the short time they'd known each other, and she'd eagerly accepted his kind offer. Two members of the crew played the wedding march on guitars as she

walked across the deck towards her fate, and the rest
of the crew had assembled to wish her well. Only
Luca's eyes were narrowed as he surveyed her. Was
he disappointed in his choice of bride?

Too bad, she thought with what little remained of
natural humour on this most daunting of days. *He's
got me now. How must Luca be feeling?* she wondered as she closed the distance between them. Was
any bride fit for a prince of his standing?

'I do,' she stated firmly when the question was
asked. This was her duty. A new life for her father
beckoned. If there could be a better outcome, she
couldn't imagine what it might be. Luca had been
very generous, both with her father's pension, and
with his wedding gift to Samia of a handwritten reassurance from the gamekeeper leading the caring
community her father would be joining on Luca's
Scottish estate. She could be confident her father
would be given the best possible chance to recover
when he was welcomed into the remote Highland
village. She glanced heavenward in what she knew
was a childish gesture, almost as if to reassure her
mother that everything would be okay now.

'I have great pleasure in pronouncing you man
and wife.'

It was done.

'You may kiss your bride…'

Luca had never seemed more imposing or more
intimidating as he brushed her lips with his. Sens-
ing the savage power within his muscular body, as
yet supremely controlled, but due to be unleashed

that same evening, she trembled. So tall he blotted out the sun, and so blisteringly masculine she felt swamped in his arms, for a moment she panicked, wondering how on earth she could go through with this marriage, and all it entailed.

'Don't be afraid, little one,' Luca whispered in her ear. 'I'll take care of you now…'

Extricating herself from his embrace with as much dignity as she could muster while they were surrounded by well-wishers, all of whom—with the possible exception of Domenico—no doubt imagined that they were witnessing a fairy-tale romance, she smiled up at him serenely.

'Thank you…' Any further commentary she might wish to make on Luca's choice of endearment could wait.

'Do you like your wedding band?'

'I love it.' Samia realised she was twirling it round and round her finger. At least one thing was right about today. The slim platinum band represented everything she believed about love and commitment. It needed no adornment. It simply was. Or was not, in this case.

'The twist of your mouth suggests otherwise,' Luca observed as they sat at a dining table set for two. He'd dismissed the stewards so they were alone on deck. 'It was better not to have a formal wedding banquet to sit through,' he'd said. He wanted to protect Samia from other people's curiosity. Conversation would be necessarily stilted between the guests, as everyone tried to get up to speed with the bride, and what had happened beneath the radar to result in this hectic wedding. They would wonder where her family was, and if anyone apart from insiders knew this was happening.

'No. Seriously. I love my wedding ring,' she assured him. 'You couldn't have chosen anything better.'

'Then, why are you so quiet?'

She stared at him levelly. 'First, even though I never took the option off the table for myself, I never actually imagined I'd ever get married again. That I did so in such a rush obviously gives me pause for thought. Then, if I'm completely honest, I always imagined that somewhere in my future I might meet someone, and love them as they loved me.'

'That's your romantic side flexing its muscles again.'

'And I'm not ashamed of it.'

'Nor should you be,' Luca said as he topped up their champagne. 'Should I have given you a chance to change your clothes?' he added as they chinked glasses.

'Into something less comfortable?' she teased weakly. 'You look uncomfortable in that formal suit, while this gown is extremely forgiving. Why don't you take your jacket off and relax?'

'Are you ordering me about?'

'Maybe…' Further conversation was halted by the sight of Luca's muscles flexing as he stood to take the jacket off, and the knowledge that, in a very short time, she would be sharing a bed with that big, powerful frame, all of which was built to scale.

'You made an excellent choice of gown.'

Instinctively, she glanced down to where the cut of her bridal gown displayed her breasts. Her ex had always said she should cover them up—

'Forget him,' Luca said, reading her with his usual ease. 'You're married to me now.'

She stared down at Luca's hand covering hers. He was right. 'I'm sorry you read my distraction so accurately.'

'There's no need to be sorry. Just accept you're beautiful and leave it at that. If I tell you often enough, you will eventually believe it.'

'And then my head will be too big to fit through the doors.'

'Don't worry. I can handle you.'

Heat rushed through her as she imagined that promise transferred to the bedroom. She might have her fears and doubts when it came to the marriage bed, but her body was wholly in favour of the idea. As she adjusted the bodice on her dress she caught Luca staring at her. He seemed to understand there was a lot of damage to repair—for both of them, she thought. Remembering how she'd bridled at his throwaway comment, 'little one,' she thought it not worth pursuing. They'd get to know each other and their boundaries gradually as they went along. To challenge him now would be petty. Shouldn't every partner in a healthy relationship want to look out for

the other? She had to get used to a new way of thinking to give this unique situation a chance of survival.

Samia was a beautiful bride. And still a largely unknown quantity. But that would change in time. At
this moment, he couldn't believe how lucky he was,
or that fickle fate had brought them together. He had
needed a bride—almost any bride would do. Then
she crossed his path. He considered that to be the
most extraordinary piece of good luck.

'You're staring at me,' she remarked with a slow-
forming smile.

'Am I?' he queried. 'I wonder why that could be.'

'I have spinach between my teeth?'

He shook his head. 'No. Because that delicate
ivory gown is the perfect foil for your hair.' Which,
since the brief ceremony, she had unpinned and
brushed out so it floated around her shoulders like
a fiery cloud.

'I've never worn anything like this before,' she
confessed as she smoothed the pale fabric.

Or taken anything like it off before, he guessed
as he pictured the moment when he would remove it
with the care and deliberation she deserved before he
kissed every inch of her naked body. The night-dark
sky was like a canopy over a throne crowned with
stars, and cloaked in the last rays of the sun. When
they returned to Madlena, there would be a blessing of this marriage for his people to witness and
then he would be enthroned with Samia at his side.

'Are you listening?' she asked.

'I have to confess, not a word,' he admitted.

She hummed in mock disapproval. 'I was saying that I have to work—a proper job. I need a purpose that goes beyond dressing up.'

Samia seemed oblivious to the fact that she had married into unimaginable wealth. 'Why don't you make a start by redesigning my properties?'

'That's hardly my forte.'

'I have plenty of properties—'

'Let me stop you there,' she said firmly. 'I'm not a practically minded person. If you want me to write a brief, or a wish list, I can do that for you, and willingly, but hands-on renovation will take a team of experts. That's not who I am, and if we're going to go forward successfully and make a positive difference to Madlena, each of us needs to play to our strengths.'

His lips tightened as he considered this, and then he shrugged. 'You're not that person,' he agreed. She was so much more, and only needed the confidence to prove it.

'What's it like to live like this?' she asked as they finished their meal.

'Complicated,' he admitted.

'Nothing's ever as straightforward as it appears, is it?' she observed. 'So, if it's all right with you, after dinner I'd like to discuss some of my ideas going forward.'

After dinner they'd be in bed.

She talked animatedly for a while, until the moment came when neither of them brought up a new topic, and he thought she looked uncomfortable, and guessed she was hunting for a reason to delay their wedding night. Pushing his chair back, he stood. She glanced up, but made no move to join him. 'I'm not tired at all,' she insisted brightly as he eased his neck.

'That's good.'

She froze.

'It's a lot to take in,' he reassured. 'So much has happened in so short a time.'

'Exactly,' she agreed, 'so why the rush?'

'You need to take a rest. It's been a busy day.' She looked at him with surprise. 'Around midday tomorrow we'll arrive in Madlena, which means we both need our sleep.'

He waited to escort her to their stateroom, but she didn't move. 'You're frightened,' he said. 'I get that.' He should understand, having read the sickening report supplied by his security team. Not only had Samia's ex-husband brutalised her, he had also secretly filmed his depravity.

'Frightened?' she scoffed weakly as she stumbled to her feet.

'Your days of fear are over,' he murmured as he linked her arm through his.

Luca was right, she was terrified of failure, and his kindness almost made it worse. They crossed the grand salon side by side, the handsome prince and his awkward bride, heading for the bridal chamber. By the time they reached the door of Luca's suite, her heart was racing so fast she could hardly breathe. Opening the door, he led the way inside. 'Make yourself at home,' he invited. 'This *is* your home now—or at least one of them.'

'But I don't have anything here,' she said, registering the fact that she sounded utterly panic-stricken for the want of a toothbrush, some nightwear and a change of clothes.

'Domenico will have anticipated your every wish,' Luca assured her with an understanding smile. 'You have your own separate dressing room and bathroom here. Please,' he offered, indicating the doors to these, 'take as long as you want.'

'But I can't…'

'Turn around,' he invited.

His fingers on the back of her neck were like incendiary devices to her senses as he began to undo the tiny buttons that ran the length of her wedding gown to the waist. It was impossible not to react as they brushed her shoulder blades. She quivered involuntarily beneath his touch. When he was finished and the gown slid from her body to pool on the floor, she was naked underneath except for a single wisp of underwear, and shivering.

'Are you cold?'

It was a warm Mediterranean night. She could hardly blame the weather for the white-hot terror surging through her veins. Another man, another wedding night, was playing like a film through her mind. Her ex had never loved her, and she knew that now, though at the time she had still believed in fairy tales. She was nothing more than a means to an end, a link in a chain that led to a weak father and the possibility of a golf course in Scotland. She'd had no idea about pleasing a man in bed, or what was expected of her—she still had no idea.

'Samia…stop it,' Luca said gently as he brought her close. 'I'm not that man.'

No. And for such a big man he could be incredibly gentle. 'I know,' she whispered on a throat so dry her tongue cleaved to the roof of her mouth.

'What do you want? What can I do to reassure you?'

Tenderness, sharing, trusting, all those things, but how to put that into words?

I want you to hold me and lay me down on a newly made bed that smells of sunshine and soap. I want to experience pleasure, but I don't think I can. I want to give you pleasure, but I don't know how. What I dread most is that you will mock me and my body. And I don't want penetration, because I know it hurts.

Sweeping her into his arms, Luca carried her to the bed. Tossing the covers back, he murmured, 'Sleep well,' as he tucked her in.

She glanced up in alarm. 'Where are you going?'

'To the gym.'

As the door closed behind him she knew she'd failed. And before she'd even got to the first hurdle. The weight of that failure pressed down on her like rocks. She lay in bed as stiff as a statue, registering each new sound in the hope that a familiar footstep might return. It didn't, of course. An hour later, there was still no sign of Luca. All she could hear was the slap of the sails and the creak of the ropes, as the wind carried them forward to a destination she could only hope would be better than this lonely place.

Reaching out, she traced the crisp, cool sheets with her fingertips. The ceaseless movement of the waves only acted as a cruel reminder that there was nothing to fear in Luca's bed. Numb and empty inside, she was a bride without a groom, a woman without a purpose. Luca couldn't have made it clearer that their marriage of convenience was just that, a formality that suited him. It would reassure his country, but he felt no obligation to take part, or to carry out his marital duties.

Which should come as a huge relief. But it didn't. Instead, it only underlined the fact that her ex had been right all along. She wasn't desirable. She was incapable of being attractive to a man. She was a failure. When they reached Madlena, how long would Luca put up with that without seeking comfort elsewhere?

What could she do about it? Lie here, feeling sorry for herself, waiting for events to unfold? What about that task she'd set herself to help Luca climb out of his grief? She wasn't going to do that by brooding alone.

Slipping out of bed, she explored the suite of rooms until she found to her pleasure that the dressing room meant for her had been stocked with brand-new clothes, none of which had come from her original dressing room. She smiled, and knew it was a kindness from Domenico. Now she turned to the sumptuous bathroom, which was fit for a princess, or a woman whose head was whirring with ideas.

Having almost destroyed the punchbag, he lifted weights until he ran out of plates to add, and then set off on the running machine for a straight ten miles uphill. Having exhausted all the possibilities for expending energy in the gym, he took an ice-cold shower that gave him the chance to ponder where he was at, and what he'd done.

Shaking sodden clumps of hair out of his eyes, he planted his fists on the wall and swore viciously. Not only did he have the uncomfortable mix of mourning a much-loved brother, and a personal reputation to salvage, he had a business to run, and a country to reassure, and now a damaged woman, one he cared deeply about, and had married, who had troubles that needing sorting right away. How to best allocate his time to each of these concerns was now his most preoccupying thought.

'Well done, Luca,' he snarled as he switched off the shower and reached for a towel. 'You've excelled yourself this time.'

One step at a time, he concluded as he tugged on his jeans. Which meant, to the great pleasure of the wolf inside him, that Samia and only Samia should be his priority tonight. But by the time he returned to their bedroom, his bride was curled in a ball, breathing at the steady pace of sleep. He stared at her for a moment and then at the couch across the room.

To hell with that!

CHAPTER SIXTEEN

SHE WOKE SLOWLY in absolute blackness, and was uncertain for a moment or two as to where she was. Reaching out her legs and arms to find a cool spot in the bed, she discovered a hot, naked body next to hers, and shot up. Now she was wide awake. Unscrambling her brain, she realised Luca had finally come to bed. Now what?

'It's two o'clock in the morning,' he growled. 'Go back to sleep.'

She couldn't decide if his lack of enthusiasm was her fault, or if he was taking a nap while he could. Angry waves were crashing against the hull, rocking the yacht, so maybe he needed to rest before returning to the business of sailing? He didn't seem unduly disturbed, she reflected as she rested on one elbow to stare down. Sprawled starfish-fashion on the bed, Luca appeared to be sleeping soundly again. How did that make her feel? Surplus to requirements? A necessary evil he'd got himself lumbered with? Maybe he already had a mistress waiting for him in Madlena. The thought pierced her heart and twisted deep like a corkscrew. However dismissive Luca might be, telling her to go to sleep on their wedding night, her feelings for him showed no sign of flagging. Yes, she still dreaded the possibility of him wanting more than she could give in bed, but not having him want anything from her was almost worse.

It was worse, she decided when Luca woke and told her once again to settle down. 'How am I supposed to do that when the boat is rocking like this?'

'I'll anchor you,' he said. 'Now, be quiet and go to sleep.'

'But I—'

'But you nothing,' he said sharply.

Which was how she came to find herself lying next to Luca, as close as it was possible to be, every inch of her naked body touching his spoon-style, her back to his front, and one of Luca's muscular legs anchoring hers, just as he had promised.

His tone should have annoyed her. Pinning her to the bed should have annoyed her more, but against all the odds she found herself gradually relaxing until, with a long sigh, she allowed herself to slip away into the darkness.

He woke to find Samia in his arms with a contented smile on her face. He brushed his lips against her cheek, and then her mouth, where he lingered before pulling back to stare down into her peaceful face. Her eyelids fluttered and then she looked up with surprise. 'Just don't ask me what I'm doing here,' he suggested dryly.

'I wasn't about to.' And then, after a few moments more, she admitted, 'I'm glad you're here. I want us to be together.'

She whispered this, holding his stare steadily. Cupping her face, he kissed her long and slow. When he judged the moment right, he brought her into his arms and drew the covers back. When she attempted to raise them again, he tossed them off the bed. 'You're beautiful. Why would you want to hide yourself?' She made a little sound, almost like a suppressed sob. He was already kissing her collarbone so she didn't see his expression turn grim. He'd arranged for lawyers to deal with her ex and they were already making great strides to bring him down. It wouldn't be too long before the man faced the justice he so thoroughly deserved. But in the meantime, they could handle it without emotion, which he doubted he could, and anger only provoked a reaction that he wouldn't risk in case it hurt Samia. She'd suffered enough unkindness for one lifetime.

Stroking her to soothe her down, he dropped kisses on her eyelids and her mouth. At first she covered herself with her arms, and crossed her legs for good measure, but gradually, with whispered inducements in his own language, he encouraged her to loosen up, and, by avoiding any particularly sensitive areas, he finally managed to win her trust. He had no inhibitions, and perhaps it was as well that his brutishly masculine frame was mostly hidden by the darkness of the room. At the same time he wanted her to know every inch of him, as he wanted to know every inch of her. 'Touch me,' he encouraged when she sighed.

She stiffened and whispered, 'I can't.'

His answer was to take her hand and wrap it around him, at least partway around him, as she would need both her hands to encompass him fully, but he judged it too soon for that. Going by the soft sounds she was making as they kissed, she wasn't frightened now. She tasted so good, so warm and womanly, and her hand on him was starting to move. Running her fingertips lightly up his shaft until she reached the smooth, rounded tip, she brought her hand slowly down again. The sensation was incredible. This was no practised seductress repeating something she'd done countless times, but a woman discovering what she could do. If he thought too much about it, his much-vaunted control would be dust.

'Do you like that?' she murmured with a smile in her voice as he moved her hand away.

'What do you think?' he asked, turning her so now he was on top of her.

'What are you doing?' she asked as he nudged his way between her thighs.

'Appreciating you… Pleasuring you,' he said as he spread her wide. 'Stroking you…'

She cried out when he said this, and thrust her hips towards him in the hunt for more contact. Cupping her buttocks, he lifted her to meet him so he could give her what she needed.

'That feels so good,' she gasped.

'If I were a betting man I'd say this feels even better…'

A cry escaped her throat, and she tensed momentarily as he took her with just the tip of his straining erection. To help her forget her fears, he added a gentle touch of his slightly roughened finger pad until she was exclaiming with pleasure and couldn't help herself.

'Oh,' she cried out with disappointment when he withdrew, so he stroked her again with the tip, without seeking entry.

'Sex doesn't have to be painful or uncomfortable. There's something wrong if it is. It's a natural process where I give you pleasure and you pay me back with more.'

'Sounds good for you.'

'It is…or it will be.'

Taking her search for more contact as his cue, he increased the friction of his finger pad.

'I can't hold on!' she cried out in panic.

'You can and you must,' he insisted calmly.

'Can't I have just a little bit more?' she asked when he pulled back again.

'If that's what you want?'

'I do!'

He gave her the tip and continued to massage her at the same time, and when she arced towards him this time, he entered just by the smallest amount, and sank a little deeper, and moved back and forth before he withdrew.

'Please,' she begged, thrusting her hips up. 'You can't leave me hanging like this.'

He could and he would. 'Not yet. Only when I'm absolutely sure I have your trust.'

'You do—you *do*!' she insisted.

'Once I'm sure, I'll take you every way you want.'

How was she supposed to hold on? 'This is cruel.'

'This is the opposite of cruel,' Luca insisted. 'This has to be right, or it won't happen. Didn't I promise to keep you safe?' he murmured as he kissed her again.

Even his voice was arousing. Everything about him was a seduction. Her senses had never been so keenly tuned. Luca knew how to keep her teetering on the edge, knowing he only had to say the word to send her tumbling over. She lay suspended in his erotic embrace; this was an experience like no other. He tempted her to let go and then withdrew the offer. She wanted to scream and shout with frustration.

'Unless you relax—'

'You'll what?' she demanded, moving restlessly in his arms. She only had to look into Luca's eyes to sense the pleasure in store. He was her ideal, with his thick, inky black hair, and pirate stubble that rasped her skin in such a surprisingly pleasurable way. His body was perfect. Hard, big, powerful, fit, he was ridiculously good-looking with his knowing eyes and his skilful touch. Luca Fortebracci was the most exciting thing that had ever happened to her, and she was aching for him now.

'Soon,' he promised as her hand reached down.

The brush of his warm, hard body against hers, how he tasted—everything about him—made her impatient for him. The clean taste of his mouth, the light salt of his body, mixed with the scent of warm, clean man, was turning this into an experience she would never forget. It was as if he was about to take her for the first time, and with all the care and tenderness she had always dreamed a man would use.

'Do you like that?' he asked as he tested her for readiness.

The slightest bit of friction was all it took to blank her mind. And his hands, long, sweeping strokes to reassure her that she was someone to be valued, rather than a creature to be used.

Having protected them both, he cupped her buttocks in one hand, while using the other to soothe and caress. Samia's thighs parted instinctively, inviting him to take her, a cue he took with the utmost care.

'Ah…yes, *yes*!' she exclaimed when he gave her the tip once more, but this time he didn't stop moving, and thrust gently inside her. Pulling out again, he noted her immediate complaint and took her again, moving a little further in this time. He repeated this as her cries grew more demanding, until finally he was lodged to the hilt. Her eyes widened as he stretched her, and her breathing became ragged, but then he moved his hips in a lazy, massaging motion until she couldn't hold on. She cried out for the longest time yet, rhythmically and fiercely demanding as her inner muscles attempted to milk him dry. The tiger claws he knew she had bit into his shoulders, and even when her release subsided into a series of milder spasms, he could still feel her inner muscles hungrily pumping him. Stroking her hair back from her face, he stared into her eyes as she breathed hectically in the aftermath of pleasure. 'More?' he enquired with amusement.

Her answer was to grip his buttocks with fingers turned to steel, and work her body hungrily against his.

It was a long night, and a surprising one in many ways. As if she'd woken from a long sleep, Samia was clearly intent on making up for lost time. That they wanted each other was never in any doubt. It was the strength of the longing they'd unleashed in one another that shocked him.

'I want you again,' she told him at one point when he was sure she was asleep. 'I want to ride you, and I want you to touch me. I want to feel you deep inside me, and here too,' she said, holding his gaze fiercely as she put her hand over her heart. 'I want to feel you here.'

His heart jerked in response. Had they both forgotten this was a marriage of convenience?

'Don't,' she said when he reached across to the nightstand. 'I don't want anything to come between us.'

He hesitated with his arm outstretched, and then shook his head, and did as he'd intended. 'I will not take advantage of you.' She'd had enough of that, and however cold-bloodedly they had embarked on this arrangement, he would not take more than he needed from Samia, which was to smooth the transition period in Madlena from his brother's rule to his. Then they would decide how to proceed. Until that time came, they could enjoy each other and nothing more.

'Is this just another deal for you—another business contract?' she suggested, pressing her lips down in anticipation of him confirming this in his usual blunt way.

'It's a lot more than that,' he admitted, 'but not enough to risk consequences neither of us are ready for.'

In spite of her turbulent past, Samia had surprised him by being a generous and inventive lover. If he hadn't been such a cynic, he might have said they were made for each other, but these were early days and he knew better than to rush things. Having discovered her fears were unfounded, she had unleashed a passion that was careless of risk. Impatient to try everything, she'd forgotten that for every action there was a consequence, and, though this marriage suited them both for a variety of reasons, there was no guarantee the arrangement would last.

'Luca,' she whispered as she mounted him, 'touch me… Take me deep.'

Now he had protected them both, he was more than happy to do whatever she wished.

CHAPTER SEVENTEEN

As she prepared to disembark the *Black Diamond* the following day, Samia felt as if she were still suspended on a gossamer cloud of amazement. It was hard to believe that, not only was she over all her fears about sex, but that with Luca they had been completely unfounded. She'd had no idea anything could feel so good, or that the giving and receiving of pleasure could bring her so close to someone.

She only wished that Luca felt the same, but he'd given no sign of increased affection, or that particular look one lover gave to another. Did last night mean nothing to him? It meant so much to her. She'd lived with fear for so long. And it was a pledge and a promise on her part that cut deep. She could no more look at another man than she could return to her old life…but did Luca feel anything? She couldn't read his face.

Oh, snap out of it! she told herself impatiently. Whatever happened next, she would throw herself into it with the utmost effort. Her feelings were a gift no one could steal, and not to be taken lightly.

'You're about to set foot in your new country. How do you feel about that?' Luca asked.

She forced something appropriate out of her mouth, and was relieved when someone else distracted him to brief him about some last-minute changes to their arrival plans. Naturally, the old doubts took the opportunity to resurface. Was she good enough? Could she do this? Now she was on the threshold of her new life, she realised that it came with no guarantees. But Luca had shown her that it was possible to feel safe and wanted, cared for and cherished by a man, and she could never thank him enough for that. He'd taken her on a voyage of discovery proving there were no boundaries where pleasure was concerned, and no restrictions when it came to trust.

She was falling in love, Samia realised as she watched Luca talking to his aide. Her husband was the only man she could ever want, or admire, or enjoy, and not because he was a prince or a billionaire, but because he'd made her whole again, and because they had fun together. She'd learned to laugh and to trust again last night, but now the business of being a prince and a ruler must take precedence. As it should, she accepted, but that couldn't stop her feeling lonely as Luca prepared to walk ahead of her to greet the crowds come to welcome him home.

The moment Luca appeared the cheers became deafening. Samia hung back, feeling out of her depth and sinking fast. It was one thing being strong when she was dealing with the familiar, but everything was new here—new country, new marriage, and with a man who might never love her back. Was she strong enough to deal with that? Only time would tell, but did she want to spend the foreseeable future aching for something she could never have?

'Samia?' Luca called, turning back to look at her with an assessing glance, as if measuring her ability to go through with it.

'Ready,' she confirmed. People had crowded the quay to see Prince Luca arrive with his bride, and, however inadequate she might be feeling, she owed it to him and to them to get over her anxiety.

'You look beautiful…and, as always, you've judged your appearance perfectly,' he murmured, clasping her hand.

Was that reassuring squeeze of her hand make-believe? Or the warmth in his eyes all for show? Lifting her chin, she smiled back. She had chosen her outfit with care to show respect for the country's recent grief. The plain grey suit, with its pale blue blouse to soften the tailoring, felt comfortable and relaxed, and she wore her hair tied back loosely—not too severe or, worse, unapproachable. Her only embellishment was her simple wedding ring and the love shining out of her eyes.

'Beautiful,' Luca confirmed with a look that heated her blood. But was there more than hunger in his look?

Don't be so ungrateful! Be satisfied with what you've got.

She could never thank him enough for introducing her to the precious joy of feeling safe, and for however long that lasted, she would cherish every moment. 'Are you sure I look all right?'

'How can you ask a question like that?' he demanded the moment they were enclosed in the royal limousine. 'I thought your days of doubt were behind you. It seems I still have a lot more work to do.'

'We both have a lot more work to do,' she admitted as he embraced her.

Their welcome in Madlena was even warmer than she had expected. The streets were lined with cheering crowds, and the cheers grew even louder when the people caught sight of their new Princess. This was her country now, with the weight of responsibility that entailed, and it made her all the more determined to do everything she could for Luca, who had lost a brother and believed he was to blame. He needed her every bit as much as she needed him.

'They're calling for their Princess,' Luca observed with pleasure.

Samia was thrilled and touched by all the smiling faces, and when she waved back, it was not a regal wave, but an enthusiastic, happy wave. It was still hard to come to terms with the fact that an accident of fate had changed her life to this degree. But it had not changed who she was, and it never would, she vowed silently. She was no better and no worse than she had been before they married.

Luca helped her out of the limousine when they arrived at the palace. Taking her hand, he led her forward to where a podium had been set out beneath a royal canopy. The reception from his people was wild as he turned to face them. It was as if the citizens of Madlena wanted to reassure him that they had grieved with him for the loss of his brother, but now they were ready to move forward, and with a magnificent prince at their head. Dressed in sombre black, as befitted his first day home in the country where his brother had died so tragically, with black diamonds flashing at the cuffs of his crisp white shirt, Luca exuded confidence and reassurance as the crowd chanted his name. And when he opened his arms as if to embrace his people, they cheered him as if they would never stop.

'Allow me to introduce you to my bride,' he said, speaking into the microphone on the podium. Turning to Samia, he brought her to his side. 'Princess Samia will serve our country as I will—'

She hadn't thought it possible for the cheers to grow even louder, but as Luca's strong, warm hand closed around hers, they did.

'This is a new beginning after the saddest of endings,' Luca promised the crowd. People fell silent at his words, remembering his brother. 'But together,' he added, his glance spanning the crowd before turning to include Samia in its warmth, 'we will take Madlena from strength to strength.'

Samia's ears were ringing with the sound of so many voices raised in support of their new Prince, but her heart ached at the thought that she was only window dressing, and could never be the love of Luca's life. She was the bride brought home to reassure his people, and to warm his bed for as long as it suited them both, but when it came to the sort of lasting love she yearned for, Luca remained unaware, and possibly uncaring, that she longed for more than a convenient deal.

'My people already love you,' Luca enthused as they left the temporary stage.

Yet they were deceiving them with this mock show of a happy marriage, she thought, cringing inside at their dishonesty as she raised a smile in response to Luca's words, but this was his day, not hers, and she had to get over it.

Their first day back in his homeland had been long and tiring for Samia. She would be relieved when he dismissed their attendants. He was looking forward to introducing his bride to their beautiful suite of rooms within the historic palace of Madlena.

He needn't have worried. The moment they walked into their apartment she exclaimed with pleasure. Staring up at the elaborately painted ceiling with its billowing white clouds, clear blue skies and plump pink cherubs circling the heavens on sunlit wings, she turned full circle with her arms outstretched, fingertips reaching out like a bird in flight. 'This is absolutely glorious,' she breathed.

'I'm glad you like it,' he said warmly. He'd always loved the painted ceiling, and believed the artwork in the palace had inspired his brother's love for design. 'It has been compared to the work of Michelangelo,' he explained, 'and is praised the world over for its excellence.'

'I'm not surprised,' she mused, but then her face fell and she looked away.

'Samia?'

'You don't have to keep up the pretence now we're alone.'

'The pretence?' he queried, frowning. 'What do you mean?'

'Our deal,' she explained. 'I realise you're going to be busy from now on, and I want to reassure you that you don't have to worry about me. I'll be fine. I'll have plenty to occupy my time while I'm here.'

'You certainly will,' he agreed, bringing her into his arms. She was tired. He must make allowances. But he couldn't wait another moment to feel her body close to his. Pressing her back against the heavy mahogany door, he kissed her hungrily, and after a moment of resistance, she kissed him back.

'What's wrong?' he queried gently as he brushed her wild red hair from her face. Her hair could never be contained for long, and however carefully she had arranged it, the lustrous locks had a will of their own. Just like Samia, he thought warmly. 'I realise this is all new and strange to you, but you will get used to it in time.'

'I am not worthy.'

He knew she was trying to make a joke of it, but the shadows were back in her eyes. 'Don't say that, not even as a joke.' Kissing her fears away was harder than he'd expected this time. So strong in so many ways, Samia was always ready to be hurt. It was as if she expected every rainbow to have a quagmire at the end of it instead of a pot of gold. Anger rose inside him as he thought again about her past, and he silently vowed that, whatever it took, he would make her whole again. 'I can't think of anyone worthier, or more fun and compassionate than you.'

'That's only because you don't know me yet,' she teased with a shrug.

'And who do you think is taking the bigger chance in this relationship?' he asked, dipping his head to stare her in the eyes. 'Me or you?'

Her eyes searched his. 'We both are,' she said softly.

'Then, let me reassure you…'

One kiss to soothe her, and another to arouse, and then he carried her across the room to the bed, by which time her arms were looped around his neck, and her legs had encircled his waist.

He couldn't restrain himself and thrust hungrily against her plumply aroused body. She cried out with pleasure. Rotating his hips, he massaged the place that craved his attention most. That was the starting gun. Reaching for his belt buckle, she made short work of his zipper. Scraps of lace went flying, and moments later he took his beautiful bride thoroughly and completely in one ecstasy-provoking plunge.

Samia had no intention of holding on and came immediately. Shrieking his name, she bucked wildly in the grip of an orgasm so powerful he had to tighten his hold on her buttocks to keep her in place as the pleasure waves rolled on and on.

'Good!' she exclaimed, collapsing against him. *'So good!'*

He kissed her to soothe her down, until finally she smiled into his eyes and asked, 'Now, can we go to bed?'

'Whatever my princess desires.'

Having discovered the pleasures of sex, it seemed Samia couldn't get enough, but this was more than sexual attraction for him, he reflected when she finally fell back on the bed groaning with contentment. This was trust and sharing, as he'd never known it before. A good sign for the future, he thought as Samia twined her legs around his and snuggled deep into his arms. 'Can we sleep a little now?' she said groggily.

'Are you finally admitting I've exhausted you?'

Her steady breathing answered the question. Princess Samia was asleep.

Every lifelong relationship had to begin somewhere, he mused as he studied her sleeping face. She looked so innocent. Her moods had run the gamut since they'd met from exuberance to anxiety, on to doubt, and then to this sleeping contentment, which he mightily preferred. It made him feel good to raise her up any way he could. Samia deserved to be happy, and he was fiercely determined to make sure she was.

He had to ask himself, was this love? What was happening to him? He'd never felt such a wealth of feeling before, or such an overwhelming desire to remain close to someone, so he could protect and grow with them for the rest of his life. This so-called marriage of convenience was already so much more, he reflected as he rested back in bed.

It was the best night's sleep she'd had in ages, but her mind remained made up. It was as though sleeping so soundly had finally reconnected the wires in her brain and she knew what she had to do. There was no going back now. Anxious not to wake Luca, who was sleeping soundly with one powerful arm thrown across his face, she crept out of bed and went to the dressing room where she dug out her old backpack and her mother's walking boots, thoughtfully placed there with the rest of her things by Domenico, who had intuited how much they meant to her. She wouldn't take anything she hadn't arrived with, with the exception of her wedding ring, which refused point-blank to budge from her finger.

'What are you doing?'

Shocked to be discovered acting furtively, she swung around to see Luca leaning against the door. 'Leaving you.'

'Leaving?'

'I can't do this. I can't look those people in the eye day after day after day and live a lie. I don't know how I ever thought I could. They deserve more than this empty marriage, and a Princess who isn't fitted for the task.'

'What the hell are you talking about?' Luca's voice was still husky with sleep, and his face was incapable of subtlety while he was only half-awake. He was angry and surprised.

'I'm leaving you,' she said again. 'It's for the best. I can play-act for a while, like anyone else, but I'd mess it up spectacularly in the end. Even you must admit, I'm hardly traditional princess material.'

'Which is exactly the point, and why you're here. I didn't want traditional—I'm not even sure what that is,' Luca growled, knuckling his eyes.

'You should take your time. Choose a bride properly, not just be landed with me because I bumped into you and suited your purpose for a few months.'

Luca's dark eyes narrowed to slits of suspicion. 'You're putting a time limit on our arrangement now?'

'It just ran out,' she fired back. 'This is an *arrangement*, which is *my point*. It's not a love match, and we both deserve more. What happens when you eventually fall in love with someone else and you can't live without them?'

'I'll certainly miss you,' he admitted, scowling deeply. 'Imagine the peaceful lie-in I'd get in the mornings.'

'But we hardly know each other,' she pointed out with exasperation.

'I'd say we know each other pretty well already,' Luca fired back. 'I can't think of any other woman I've been on such a rapid journey with, and I can't say I appreciate hearing that you've taken nothing from it apart from physical gratification.'

'That's not true!' She flared up. 'How dare you turn this around on me?'

'You've just decided our marriage has a sell-by date.'

'You decided that first. It was for five years, you told me. It was never meant to last for ever.'

'Well, maybe I changed my mind,' he growled. 'I hope you're not suggesting I'm as dishonest and manipulative as your ex? I thought we arrived at this agreement together, and that it was for our *mutual* benefit?'

'A straightforward business transaction is what you called it.'

'And now that's not enough. Maybe what has happened since I said that is too much for you? Please,' he said, throwing his arms wide. 'Enlighten me.'

'I don't know what it takes to be a princess, but I'm pretty sure I don't have it,' she insisted stubbornly.

'Just be yourself. That's all anyone would expect from you.'

'I don't know who that is anymore,' she wailed.

'Then, perhaps you should leave,' he said coolly. 'If you can't leave the past with all its doubts and demons behind, then maybe I'd be better off without you.'

'You would be. As I would be better off without you, because you can't leave the past behind, either, and the sooner you come to terms with that, the happier you'll be. You've said you let your brother down. I believe I let my mother down, when the truth is, we loved them with all our hearts, and would have done anything to make things better for them, but what I've come to realise is, they each left us, not the other way around. I'm right about that, aren't I? About Pietro?'

There was a long silence, and then Luca nodded and said quietly, 'When did you get to be so wise?'

'When I met you and started seeing things as they were, rather than as I dreamed they might be—which was rather terrifying when I discovered you were the infamous Pirate Prince.'

'So why can't you see things as they are now—this minute—right here, right now? You are a princess. Suck it up.'

'Are you kidding? I mean, look at me.'

'You look beautiful to me, though those boots could do with some loving attention from a tin of polish.'

She was still riled up inside, but relieved at the same time that the crisis seemed to be over, and they could part as friends, as she'd hoped. 'This is me,' she said, running a hand down her shabby clothes. This is who I really am. I'll never make a suitable Princess for you. Even you can't fit a round peg into a square hole.'

'No,' Luca admitted thoughtfully, 'but I know someone who can.'

'Who?'

'Not now,' he murmured. 'I've got something else on my mind.'

'What?' Samia shook her head in disbelief. 'Isn't

this situation serious enough for you to spare time to discuss it?'

'It certainly is,' he murmured, tapping his stubbled chin with a long finger.

'So, what is this something else?' she asked, weakening with curiosity, even though she knew she should stick to her guns.

'You,' he said wickedly, yanking her close.

CHAPTER EIGHTEEN

AFTER A LONG lie-in and a lazy shower, which involved more activity than the term 'lazy' might suggest, he told Samia to give him the chance to prove she was indeed the perfect Princess for him and for their people.

She insisted on wearing her original travel clothes, while he wore jeans to take her on the back of his Harley to the artists' quarter in town. A tall, undistinguished building occupied most of a cobbled square, and, dismounting from the beast, they jogged up five flights of stairs until they reached the penthouse floor.

'Wow,' she gasped when they walked in.

'I guess the word *penthouse* hardly conjures up the reality of this place,' he admitted. The entire top floor had been knocked into one massive room that could be used for a variety of purposes. 'It's an artists' commune,' he explained. 'Everyone has their own space for however long they need it. They can even sleep here, if they want, and they all have the very best of sponsors in my beloved *nonna*.'

'Your grandmother is a patron of the arts?'

'And an artist in her own right,' he revealed. 'She undertook the restoration of the ceilings in the palace with a team of fellow craftsmen. At almost seventy years old, she lay on her back on top of the scaffold, painting for months.'

'Like Michelangelo! She must be fit—'

'Creaking a little these days, my dear...'

'Nonna!' Swinging around, Luca exchanged the warmest of hugs with a tiny, birdlike woman whose arms barely stretched around his waist. Her abundant grey hair was held up with a couple of paintbrushes, and she was dressed in a shapeless artist's smock, of indeterminate colour beneath a blizzard of paint smears. Her face was old and wise, her smile wide, and her raisin-black eyes full of warmth as they fixed on Samia's with the friendliest of greetings.

'Luca, my naughty boy,' she exclaimed, stepping back from the giant towering over her. 'Why have you stayed away so long?'

'Because, as you told me to, Nonna, I've been searching for a bride.'

'As if you'd do anything I told you to,' his grandmother scoffed. 'But here she is,' she added in a softer tone. Stepping back, she took a shrewd look at Samia. 'Well, Luca, are you going to introduce us?'

'Of course. Princess Aurelia, may I present my wife...?'

'Samia,' Samia broke in, bobbing a curtsey. 'Just plain Samia.'

This comment produced a hearty guffaw from a woman who looked as if a puff of wind would blow her over. 'A kindred spirit! I knew it at once. This isn't one of your painted trollops, Luca, or a namby-pamby milksop, but a down-to-earth woman with sensible boots. How are you, my dear?'

It was Samia's turn for a warm hug. Wrestling with the sharp tang of turpentine overlaid with carbolic soap, she laughed as Luca's grandmother demanded, 'Are you in charge of this man? Keep him on a short leash. I couldn't bear any harm to come to him. He has my heart. Luca *is* my heart.' Returning her attention to her grandson, she adopted a stern face that wasn't quite as successful as maybe she had intended. 'Bad boy. Why did it take so long to come to your senses?'

'Perfect princesses don't grow on trees?' Luca suggested, cocking his head to one side to bathe his grandmother in the warmth of his smile.

'And if they did you'd probably stride past them, silly boy. I imagine Samia bumped into you? Am I right?'

They both stared at her, and then they laughed. 'How did you know?' Samia asked as the princess linked arms to draw her deeper into the busy space where at least half a dozen artists were working, each lost in their work.

'Because Luca feeds off the unexpected, and I can see from the way he looks at you that he's madly in love.'

Samia blinked. 'You can?'

'Of course! How can you doubt it? My grandson never does anything by halves, and the fact that he's brought you to meet me speaks volumes.'

'I'm just not sure that I—'

'Can be a princess?' Princess Aurelia supplied. 'That's what I thought once upon a time. You can see I'm hardly conventional. But if you care for someone—really care—you can expand your heart to encompass everything they care about, even when that means embracing an entire country and its people. The citizens of Madlena need someone like you, as they needed me in my time, to reassure them that their royal family is just as delightfully quirky as theirs. As far as I'm concerned,' she added, smiling into Samia's eyes, 'I'm delighted to welcome you into our family.'

'So what did you think of the last Princess of Madlena?' Luca asked when they arrived back at the palace. Having parked the Harley in the vast courtyard at the back of the building, they strolled through the exquisitely manicured gardens to their apartment.

'I think your grandmother is absolutely amazing,' Samia admitted as they paused in the shade of a rose arbour, where swags of pink roses exuded the most exquisite scent. 'It would be impossible not to love her. You must be very proud.'

'I am,' Luca confessed. 'She helped to bring me up, though she thought I'd be better off with my brother after she was widowed and her life started gravitating towards the artists' community she'd created. Pietro would soften me, she said, while she might lead me astray with her bohemian lifestyle, which in her opinion was the last thing I needed.'

'She's a wonderful woman.'

'And a wonderful princess, adored by the people of Madlena. They see her strength and love her for her eccentricity, and they know her to be deeply caring. She'll do anything in her power to help them, and proves it every year by donating all the proceeds of her work to Madlenan charities. She's a very different type of royal as you and I will be. I'm not going to ask you again if you want to go on this journey with me,' he added as he drew Samia into his arms. 'I'm going to tell you that I'd be nothing without you. I'd be all steel and no heart. You're the love of my life, Princess Samia, and though I'm not too good at expressing things, because I've never felt this way before, I can promise that I'll tell you that I love you again and again.'

'Please do,' she whispered, staring up into Luca's eyes.

'I love you and I want you at my side. You're not just a princess who is more than worthy of the name, you're the woman I adore, and will do for the rest of my life.'

'Love,' she whispered, loving the sound of that word. It made all the difference in the world.

'Adore,' Luca countered. Adopting a thoughtful

expression, he added, 'You *love* hamburgers, but I'll give you every reason to adore me.'

'I love *and* adore you.'

'No more than I adore you,' he said.

EPILOGUE

A year later...

THE FORMAL BLESSING of Luca and Samia's marriage was held on Prince Pietro's Day. Starting from this day, Luca's late brother would be honoured every year with an annual public holiday.

The glorious medieval cathedral in Madlena with its soaring vaulted ceiling was bathed in jewelled light streaming through the stained-glass windows. Guests from all walks of life had gathered to celebrate an outstanding first year for Prince Luca and Princess Samia. Not only was the country riding the crest of a wave thanks to the tireless marketing of its many assets by a talented princess who used the home-grown artwork of her grandmother-in-law's artists' collective to enhance her promotion of the country, but Princess Samia was pregnant, which was a cause for general rejoicing.

Domenico insisted on escorting Samia down the length of the aisle to where her handsome prince was waiting, while Princess Aurelia, dressed for the occasion in diamonds and ankle-length shocking pink silk-satin, stood on her other side. Glorious organ music accompanied them, while the scent of white roses filled the air.

'Much as it pains me to hand you back to this brute of a man,' Domenico murmured as they reached the steps of the altar, 'I have to say, you've improved him a little, but there's still a lot of work to do.'

'A lifetime of work, I hope,' Luca remarked dryly.

Samia's heart swelled with love as she stared up at the handsome prince at her side. In his official regalia of black and gold, with a red silk-satin sash of office pinned with a magnificent jewel running diagonally across his powerful chest, Luca was… quite simply, the man she loved. He had restored her confidence in every way, and set her free to fly. *Which only goes to prove*, she reflected, *that even when a bird flies free, it still returns to those it loves.*

As Domenico and Princess Aurelia melted back into the congregation, Luca stared deep into her eyes. 'You look beautiful…*again*,' he murmured.

The smile they exchanged was both intimate and perfect. Samia's elegant peach-coloured gown was cut cunningly to flatter, rather than to hide her growing bump. They were both so thrilled about the tiny prince or princess that they celebrated constantly— often in the most unlikely places. Who knew a palace had so many nooks and crannies for a love-struck couple to hide away?

'That gown is gorgeous,' Luca said huskily. 'I can't wait to take it off you.'

'Shh!' Samia implored as the thundering organ quietened.

But, with its lace bandeau bodice and filmy long sleeves, it was a fairy-tale dress. It had arrived as a surprise from Paris. 'So you can't refuse to wear it!' Luca had teased his practical bride.

When she'd lifted the filmy creation from its reams of tissue paper, the gown had taken her breath away.

'And I want you to wear this too,' Luca had said as he'd produced the priceless fringe tiara of sparkling blue-white diamonds that had once belonged to his late mother. 'You'll have to take that off before I make love to you,' he murmured discreetly now. 'Or we'll end the night in the ICU.'

'You're *so* romantic,' Samia remarked with loving irony as the service began.

'Aren't I just?' Luca agreed. 'But I'd do it all *again*,' he insisted.

'And again, I hope,' she murmured back, 'because I love you.'

'As I love you,' Luca responded, smiling into her eyes. 'With all my heart, and my body too…'

'What a coincidence,' she said as Domenico cleared his throat theatrically to draw their attention to the fact that the service had begun, 'because I adore you too, and I always will.'

'Ditto,' Luca mouthed with a wink for Domenico.

* * * * *

WE HOPE YOU ENJOYED
THIS BOOK FROM
⬥ HARLEQUIN
PRESENTS

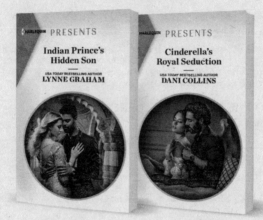

Escape to exotic locations where passion knows no bounds.

Welcome to the glamorous lives of royals and billionaires, where passion knows no bounds. Be swept into a world of luxury, wealth and exotic locations.

8 NEW BOOKS AVAILABLE EVERY MONTH!

#3813 A HIDDEN HEIR TO REDEEM HIM
Feuding Billionaire Brothers
by Dani Collins
Kiara could never regret the consequence of her one delicious night with Val—despite his coldheartedness. Yet behind Val's reputation is another man—revealed only in their passionate moments alone. Could she give *that* man a second chance?

#3814 CROWNING HIS UNLIKELY PRINCESS
by Michelle Conder
Cassidy's boss, Logan, is about to become king! She's busy trying to organize his royal diary—*and* handle the desire he's suddenly awakened! But when Logan reveals he craves her, too, Cassidy must decide: Could she *really* be his princess?

#3815 CONTRACTED TO HER GREEK ENEMY
by Annie West
Stephanie would love to throw tycoon Damen's outrageous proposal back in his face, but the truth is she must save her penniless family. Their contract says they can't kiss again...but Steph might soon regret that clause!

#3816 THE SPANIARD'S WEDDING REVENGE
by Jackie Ashenden
Securing Leonie's hand in marriage would allow Cristiano to take the one thing his enemy cares about. His first step? Convincing his newest—most *defiant*—employee to meet him at the altar!

YOU CAN FIND MORE INFORMATION ON UPCOMING HARLEQUIN TITLES, FREE EXCERPTS AND MORE AT HARLEQUIN.COM.

HPCNMRB0420

"No." He held on to her wrist as though he could tell she was
about to run from the room. "Stop."

Her eyes lifted to his and she jerked on her wrist so she could
lift her fingers to her eyes and brush away her tears. Panic was
filling her, panic and disbelief at the mess she found herself in.

"How is this upsetting to you?" he asked more gently,
pressing his hands to her shoulders, stroking his thumbs over her
collarbone. "We agreed at the hotel that we could only have two
nights together, and you were fine with that. I'm offering you three
months on exactly those same terms, and you're acting as though
I've asked you to parade naked through the streets of Shajarah."

"You're ashamed of me," she said simply. "In New York we
were two people who wanted to be together. What you're proposing
turns me into your possession."

He stared at her, his eyes narrowed. "The money I will give you
is beside the point."

More tears sparkled on her lashes. "Not to me it's not."

"Then don't take the money," he said urgently. "Come to the
RKH and be my lover because you want to be with me."

"I can't." Tears fell freely down her face now. "I need that
money. I need it."

A muscle jerked in his jaw. "So have both."

"No, you don't understand."

She was a live wire of panic but she had to tell him, so that he understood why his offer was so revolting to her. She pulled away from him, pacing toward the windows, looking out on this city she loved. The trees at Bryant Park whistled in the fall breeze and she watched them for a moment, remembering the first time she'd seen them. She'd been a little girl, five, maybe six, and her dad had been performing at the restaurant on the fringes of the park. She'd worn her very best dress and, despite the heat, tights that were so uncomfortable she could vividly remember that feeling now. But the park had been beautiful and her dad's music had, as always, filled her heart with pleasure and joy.

Sariq was behind her now; she felt him, but didn't turn to look at him.

"I'm glad you were so honest with me today. It makes it easier for me, in a way, because I know exactly how you feel, how you see me and what you want from me." Her voice was hollow, completely devoid of emotion when she had a thousand feelings throbbing inside her.

He said nothing. He didn't try to deny it. Good. Just as she'd said, it was easier when things were black-and-white.

"I don't want money so I can attend Juilliard, Your Highness." It pleased her to use his title, to use that as a point of difference, to put a line between them that neither of them could cross.

Silence. Heavy, loaded with questions. And finally, "Then what do you need such a sum for?"

She bit down on her lip, her tummy squeezing tight. "I'm pregnant. And you're the father."

Don't miss
The Secret Kept from the King,
available May 2020 wherever
Harlequin Presents books and ebooks are sold.

Harlequin.com

4188

Love Harlequin romance?

DISCOVER.

Be the first to find out about promotions,
news and exclusive content!

Facebook.com/HarlequinBooks

Twitter.com/HarlequinBooks

Instagram.com/HarlequinBooks

Pinterest.com/HarlequinBooks

ReaderService.com

EXPLORE.

Sign up for the Harlequin e-newsletter and
download a free book from any series at
TryHarlequin.com

CONNECT.

Join our Harlequin community to
share your thoughts and connect
with other romance readers!
Facebook.com/groups/HarlequinConnection

 HARLEQUIN

HSOCIAL2020